Royal
Dance

BOOKS BY RACHEL BRANTON

Lily's House Series
House Without Lies
Tell Me No Lies
Hearts Never Lie
Your Eyes Don't Lie
Broken Lies
No Secrets or Lies
Cowboys Can't Lie

Finding Home Series
Take Me Home
All That I Love
Then I Found You

Other
How Far

Town Called Forgotten
Kiss at Midnight
This Feeling for You
Reason to Breathe

Royals of Beaumont
Royal Kiss
Royal Quest
Royal Dance
Royal Time

Picture Books
I Don't Want To Eat Bugs
I Don't Want to Have Hot Toes

UNDER THE NAME TEYLA BRANTON

Unbounded Series
The Change
The Cure
Protectors
  Ava's Revenge
  Mortal Brother
  Set Ablaze
The Escape
The Reckoning
Lethal Engagement
The Takeover
The Avowed

Other
Times Nine

Imprints Series
First Touch (prequel)
Touch of Rain
On The Hunt
Upstaged
Under Fire
Blinded
Street Smart
Hidden Intent
Checked In

Colony Six Series
Insight (prequel)
Sketches
Visions
Travels

Royal Dance

RACHEL
BRANTON

WHITE
STAR
PRESS

This is a work of fiction, and the views expressed herein are the sole responsibility of the author. Likewise, certain characters, places, and incidents are the product of the author's imagination, and any resemblance to actual persons, living or dead, or actual events or locales, is entirely coincidental.

Royal Dance (Royals of Beaumont, Book 3)

Published by White Star Press

Printed in the United States of America
ISBN: 978-1-948982-33-7w
Year of first printing: 2022
Year of first electronic publication 2018

Fairy tales in the kingdom of
Beaumont are real ...

Chapter 1

Harper

I stared at my reflection in the mirror, not really seeing anything, trying to pretend I didn't care that I'd be going to the engagement ball without a date. More pointedly, I'd be attending without my fiancé, who somehow managed to get his leave revoked earlier this week. Graham was stationed in Germany, and we'd seen each other only three times in the past four months since I'd been in Beaumont. The last time was a month ago when my best friend Amelia Lennox—or Mel as we called her—had insisted on sending me to Germany on her future husband's private jet.

"If Graham could see you now, he'd be begging you not to go tonight in fear that someone will steal you away," Mel said as she lifted her blond hair to fasten a sapphire necklace her fiancé, Damien Giraud, Comte de Laval, had given her last week. We were in Mel's guest suite at Damien's mansion getting ready for her engagement party, and it was hard not to feel a little like we'd stepped into a fairy tale.

I turned to admire my figure in the dress I'd helped design. The silvery gauze layer over the main gold dress hid my imperfections exactly as I'd planned. Not everyone could be as thin as Mel. I particularly liked how the dress clung to my waist before curving out in all its fullness and layers.

"It did turn out well," I admitted, "and I like the way Felisa did my hair. Whoever thought I could pull off ringlets?" Instead of the single thick coil of darkness my hair normally insisted on forming, it piled on my head in messy perfection, emphasized by said ringlets, which were apparently all the rage now in Beaumontian high society.

"They're perfect." Mel came up to stand beside me. "You look amazing."

"I'm not the only one. When Damien sees you, he's going to faint before he makes the official announcement of your engagement. That dress is the exact blue of your eyes."

"It's Damien's favorite." Mel actually giggled. She'd never been a giggler in all the years we'd been roommates at Stanford, but she was completely and utterly in love for the first time in her life, and she was giddy with the feelings.

That's the way I felt about Graham—or usually did when I wasn't upset with him. And I *was* upset. But his decision not to come to this party after we'd planned his trip so carefully was only the tiniest bit of why my heart felt frozen now whenever I thought of him.

"Stop that." Mel tapped my shoulder. "Frowns aren't allowed today. I endured you getting engaged; now it's my turn. Come on, pose for me. I'm going to take a picture to send to Graham later."

"Why bother? We'll be in all the gossip columns tomorrow."

She laughed. "There is that. But Graham doesn't exactly follow that sort of thing."

That was true. I was always poring over the latest magazines and even newspaper articles with the hope of seeing decorating tips before they became all the rage, but Graham was more interested in airplanes and military maneuvers—part of the reason he was in Germany in the first place. He'd been assigned to military intelligence in Wiesbaden, which sounded great but also meant he'd be stuck there for another few years. Germany wasn't at all how I'd planned to spend my first years as a married woman, but it was better than waiting to finally be married. At least now that I was in Beaumont, we were only an hour apart by plane and seven hours by car. Not that the relative closeness had stopped us from having problems.

"I said no frowning!"

I smoothed my forehead as Mel snapped a picture with her phone. Then she put her arms around me. "I know it stinks that he's not here, but in a few months you two will be married, and this separation will be behind you."

I hugged her back. "You're right. It's just hard."

"I know. I think I would die if I was separated from Damien that long, but you're stronger than I am."

I faked a stoic expression. "You do what you have to."

I didn't feel as if I would die without Graham, so maybe I *was* stronger than I thought. Or maybe my heart still needed to heal from the hurt he'd put me through. Anyway, if I'd stayed home in America pining for him or had pushed up our wedding, I'd have never experienced Beaumont with Mel—and this gorgeous little country nestled near the French border between Switzerland and Germany was worth the temporary separation. The pastries alone were worth the trip.

That didn't mean I wanted to be the third wheel at Mel's party, but at least our friend Emerson Shaw would also be at the engagement ball. Maybe I could get in a dance or two with him—if I could entice him away from Damien's younger sister, his current infatuation.

Mel hooked her arm through mine as we left the room and tried to glide down the hall the way Damien's mother, Lucida, had taught us. "Countesses and their friends don't simply walk," she'd said. However, we weren't good at gliding, and by the time we reached the top of the main staircase, we were laughing at the ridiculousness of our attempts.

Strains from the live orchestra reached our ears, and already the family and staff were gathered to meet the guests who would soon arrive, guests who would include Mel's sister Kami and her husband Gabriel, the king and queen of Beaumont. This meant security was beefed up and that nearly everyone who had status in society would be in attendance.

As I predicted, Damien's golden eyes widened and didn't leave Mel from the second we began our descent on the staircase. He took her hands as we reached the bottom and pulled her close, whispering something in her ear. She flushed and pressed her cheek against his as he bent over her. They were so right together that it made something inside me ache.

Lucida put a hand on my shoulder. "My dear, you look stunning."

"Thank you. I kind of miss the retro look, though." For our first ball nearly four months ago, Lucida had lent us her old ball gowns. Not one reporter had yet to uncover that little secret, although Mel and I didn't really care if they did.

Lucida laughed. "Retro does have a certain flair, but this design is particularly flattering on you. I think Mel should get your input on her wedding dress."

"I did offer and she accepted, but she could wear a burlap bag and she'd still look great."

Lucida nodded. "That is true." She glanced at Mel with a look of mingled pride and admiration.

Mel was lucky to have Lucida as a future in-law, and in a very real way I'd gained Lucida too. My own mother was sweet but occupied with traveling these days, and Graham's no-nonsense mother, a colonel in the army, thought me frivolous after I tried to brighten her extremely dull office with a few decorative accents.

The guests began arriving, and I started to move away, but Lucida clamped her hands on my arm. "Stay with me. I would like to introduce you to our guests. Damien will be busy showing off Mel as he greets them, and it will help to have company as I wait my turn. It appears my lovely daughter has deserted me."

Leave it to Lucida to make me feel as if I were doing her a favor. "I would be happy to meet your friends."

Damien and Mel were standing at the start of the reception line to greet the guests, followed directly by Lucida and me. The attendees already knew the reason for the party, but that only meant more were in attendance. After the Royal wedding and coronation last December, this was the next big event for Beaumont nobility. The paparazzi was already gathering outside, cameras flashing.

Not everyone was happy about Damien's engagement, however. Some of the mothers with eligible daughters appeared disgruntled as they greeted us, and one red-faced woman in a too-tight ball gown actually harrumphed when Lucida introduced me.

"I hope you aren't also here to steal all our young men," she said in heavily accented English.

The challenge in her voice was unmistakable. I should draw off my long glove to show my engagement ring, but instead I trilled, "Oh, no. Certainly not all of them. What would I do with more than one?"

Next to me, Lucida twitched, and when I glanced at her, I saw she was trying hard not to smile. The other woman stalked off, muttering something under her breath to her young daughter, who was actually rather pleasant. My French was still too rusty to know what she was saying, but the evil look she cast back at me didn't need translation.

The guests continued arriving, most of them gracious and polite, and Lucida handled them with ease. I found the process more interesting than tedious, though poor Mel occasionally shot me a bleak look. She was out of her comfort zone, but at least her French, the native tongue of Beaumont, was better than mine.

Then I saw a man enter through the double doors of the reception room, a man who stood out from the crowd. It wasn't so much his dark looks—most residents of Beaumont had dark hair and eyes—but rather the way he carried himself. He looked like royalty.

An older, stylish woman with dark hair piled high on her head clung to his arm as they chatted with Damien and Mel. My friend was laughing and talking to him animatedly, as she hadn't with most of the other guests, and I wondered who he could be. We were almost always together, but I would have remembered this man if we'd met before.

Lucida caught my questioning stare. "That's Prince Tristan Fontaine, Duc de Vallée, and his mother Princess Rosina Toussaint Fontaine. He's one of Gabriel's cousins."

Of course he was. The king of Beaumont had dozens of cousins and second cousins, and I'd met so many of them during the time we spent with Mel's sister at the palace that their faces all blurred in my mind. Still, I was sure I hadn't met this man. For one, he was older than the others—at least in his thirties—and he was inches taller, with shoulders broad enough to impress even me.

When they finally left Damien and Mel, Lucida met them with real pleasure. "It's so good of you to come."

Princess Rosina laughed. "Of course we wouldn't miss it," she replied in proper British English. "As I am the king's aunt, Amelia is our family too, and you and Damien have always been like family. I'm glad it's official now. I only regret that my husband cannot be here this evening. Events like this are still too taxing for him."

"I'm so sorry about his cancer." Lucida gripped the other woman's hand more tightly.

"He's going to be fine," Rosina said. "And now that he has been forced to retire, we plan to have a little more fun. It helps that Gabriel has become king. My husband understands that it's time to give the younger generation an opportunity to show us what they can do." Her eyes slid toward her son. "Now we just need this one to find a wife."

Prince Tristan's laugh was warm. "Not a problem, Mother. I will be pleased to marry as soon as I find a woman as wonderful as you."

Rosina gave a delicate snort. "You see what I am up against?"

"I do. In fact, I remember it quite well with my own son." Lucida paused, her hand touching my arm. "But please, allow me to introduce the closest friend of my future daughter-in-law: Harper Thackery."

I accepted the princess's hand, noting that both Fontaines must have already guessed at my identity because they had been speaking English. Most of the other guests had chatted with Lucida in French before my introduction, and I appreciated the Fontaines' politeness.

Tristan took my gloved hand and, to my surprise, brought it up to kiss, giving me a little bow that might have made me swoon if I weren't already taken. "A pleasure to meet you," he said. If we'd been in America, I would have laughed at his formal manner, but here at this formal engagement ball, with his accent and those sincere brown eyes, it was exactly right.

"And you." I wanted to ask how he knew Mel, but it didn't seem appropriate to admit that I'd been watching him.

Lucida and his mother turned to chat with a newcomer, but Prince Tristan remained in place, his hand still holding mine. "I hope you are enjoying our little country."

"It's beautiful. Amazing, actually."

His dark eyes studied my face as if trying to gauge my sincerity. "Will you give me the honor of a dance later?"

In another world, I would have been thrilled to say yes. I would have dreamed about the possibility of his liking me, of finding my prince. But in this world, I was committed to another man, and even if Graham hadn't always been faithful to me, I had to make sure this prince knew I was off limits.

"I would be happy to dance with you, but since my fiancé isn't here, I think I'll pass on the dancing tonight." I told myself my heart was beating faster because I hated to disappoint him. The warmth of his touch, radiating through my glove, certainly couldn't have caused the reaction.

"Ah, you're taken." Did his eyes hold regret? "I should have guessed as much. A beautiful woman like yourself." He finally released my hand, and for a brief instant, I wished he hadn't. "I guess this is goodbye then."

His eyes still watched me as he started to turn away. "Or maybe," he said, pausing, "this is actually an opportunity." He cast a quick glance at his mother, his voice lowering. "Would it be too awful to dance with a new friend who could use a little inter-ference with his match-making mother? You know that's the only reason they keep having these events, right?"

I laughed at his earnest expression. "I thought this one was to celebrate Damien and Mel's engagement."

"Ah, that's the excuse. The *real* reason is to pair off the rest of us. Otherwise it would have been a simple dinner."

"But dancing's fun," I couldn't resist saying.

"All the more reason you should dance with me. Your fiancé will have no cause to be concerned. I promise to be a complete gentleman."

Once more, I felt the urge to say yes. "Of course you would."

Would a few dances betray Graham? People danced with friends all the time, just as I'd planned to dance with Emerson. After all, this wasn't a nightclub where people draped themselves over each other like a second skin, but a classy, upscale event where ballroom dancing was the norm. If our roles were reversed, I wouldn't want Graham to sit on the sidelines if he and his buddies attended a dance.

Except that wasn't exactly true. I *would* want him to sit on the sidelines, because the draped-all-over-each-other clubs were the only kind his military buddies visited.

I sighed, wondering how to refuse again, but Tristan was already giving me that royal nod. "If you change your mind, you know where to find me."

No pushing or forcefulness—a perfect gentleman as he'd promised.

Sigh.

I couldn't help but stare after him, and I wasn't the only one. More than a few female eyes were fixed on him as he made his way into the ballroom.

I looked down at the hand he'd kissed and wished things were different.

Tristan

*A*nother blasted ball where I'd have to dance and make small talk with women who didn't interest me. Yet I hadn't been able to tell my mother no. She wanted so much for me to be happy, to go forward with my personal life and find someone to marry. As the oldest son, it was my responsibility.

And I'd fulfill that duty, but not tonight.

I needed a rest from women after my breakup with Jianne. I'd thought we'd be together forever, but I'd been wrong, and I wasn't ready yet to offer my heart to another woman—not until I figured out what went wrong the last time. I had a sneaking suspicion it was my fault our relationship hadn't worked out, and not Jianne's.

Would Jianne be here tonight? I hoped not, but we ran in the same circles, and it was a possibility.

The reception line finally broke up after Gabriel and Kami arrived fashionably late. The dancing began, and already the stares in my direction had intensified. Not only the stares from

young women, but from their mothers. Particularly, there was
a red-faced lady with a daughter who looked barely old enough
to have finished high school. They were staring pointedly in my
direction, and I steeled myself for their approach. Etiquette would
demand that I dance with the girl. Poor thing; it wasn't her fault.
I'd have to please her mother enough that she wouldn't embarrass
the child in public.

Here they come.

A hand on my arm drew my attention, and I turned to see
Harper Thackery, the American with the smile that did funny
things to my stomach and whose pale blue eyes were different
from any woman's I'd ever seen. I couldn't help the chuckle that
erupted from my mouth. "You?"

"You're right," Harper said. "Friends can dance together. And
I'd love to dance. If you still want to."

Oh, did I want to—and not just to ward off the others, though
that had been my original intent.

She's engaged, I reminded myself.

Or was she? Maybe she was playing hard to get. If so, she had
a surprise coming. I didn't like games. Of course, I couldn't refuse
her invitation any more than I could have rejected the red-faced
woman and her daughter, who had hesitated in their approach
now that I already had company. At least I was off the hook for
the moment.

"My pleasure." I put my hand over Harper's where it lay on
my arm and was almost startled to feel the engagement ring on
her finger beneath the glove. So she hadn't lied. Then what had
changed her mind about dancing with me?

As we passed the red-faced woman on our way to the dance
floor, Harper smiled at the girl, and I understood. Harper was
doing it for the girl, not for me. I found myself smiling again.
Maybe I could convince her to stay with me for more than one

dance. That way, as long as she kept her glove on to hide the ring, I could relax and try to enjoy myself, please my mother, and stave off all the other potentials at the same time.

Sliding one hand onto her waist, I pulled her into the waltz. Instantly, it was clear that Harper knew how to dance, probably better than I did. But Harper didn't just dance, she *danced.* Little flourishes and movements had me trying to remember all the variations I'd learned throughout years of lessons that were required of all noble gentlemen in Beaumont. Nothing I did surprised her. She kept up, step for step, easily following my lead, even when I threw in unexpected turns or the occasional unplanned dip. She was fluid, the most natural partner I'd ever had. Each time the music ended, neither of us moved away.

Over the years, I'd become adept at the waltz, but I'd never really enjoyed it.

Until tonight.

"You really do love to dance," I said when the strains of the fifth song wound to an end. I tried not to notice the way her chest heaved in her delicate dress, or how her intricately arranged hair begged me to touch and explore.

Off limits, I reminded myself.

"I was on the dance team during my freshman year in college, but I wasn't as dedicated as some of the others, so I gave it up."

"Not completely, I hope."

"Oh, no. I dance every chance I get."

"Your fiancé also dances?"

She nodded. "Yes. Not as well as you do, though."

For some reason I couldn't define, that knowledge pleased me. The music was beginning again, calling as it never had before, tempting me to put my arms around her. But she was still breathing deeply and the bare skin on her neck glistened with moisture, so my manners kicked in. "Would you like a drink?"

"Yes, very much. Thank you."

I offered her my arm. "No, thank *you*. I do believe we've scared off that woman and her very young daughter."

Harper laughed. "So you did notice them."

"Oh yes. It happens at all these events."

She rolled her eyes. "What a hardship."

I snagged two drinks from a passing waiter, handing one to her. "Well, when you put it that way, it sounds ridiculous. But it is a challenge being a piece of meat."

"I'll bet. A terrible, terrible challenge." She downed the drink with more gusto than my usual dates, but she obviously wasn't trying to impress me. "And I'm assuming you're a rich piece of meat, given the fact that you're a prince *and* a duke. Gee, if you had it any harder, you'd have to hire a fake girlfriend to fight them off."

I laughed again, something I'd been doing a lot of tonight with this American girl. "Well, that's not an entirely bad idea. I'm not looking for a relationship just yet."

She cocked her head, staring at me, causing one of her ringlets to fall over her right eye. I lifted a hand to move it away but drew back before actually touching her. That was too familiar, given that we'd barely met—plus she was engaged. What was it about her that made me forget myself?

"Is it because of your dad?" she asked, either not noticing or pretending not to see my gaffe. "I hope he really is getting well."

"He is, but that's not the reason." My father's illness was a big part of why my mother was pushing me to start dating again. She wanted to travel more and didn't like the idea of me living alone when she wouldn't be around to drop in as often to check on my welfare. But I didn't need to share that bit of information. "Would you like to dance again?"

Harper arched a brow. "What I really need is some water. That fruity thing we drank only made me more thirsty."

I got the hint. She'd done me a favor and was finished with me. In light of my physical attraction to her, it was probably for the best. I wondered if enough time had passed that I could sneak away from the party, maybe go for a walk and then swing by later to accompany my mother back to her hotel. I dipped my head toward Harper, intending to make it easy for her to dump me. "Maybe I'll see you later."

"Or you can come with me. It's not far to the kitchen."

Warmth spread through my chest. "The waiters probably have water."

"Yeah, but the way we've been dancing, we'd have to down four of those little cups to get enough. Come on." She grabbed my hand and led me out of the ballroom. I wondered if my mother was watching. I hoped so. It might put her worries to rest for a few weeks, unless Lucida told her Harper was already engaged.

Harper didn't take me to the main kitchen but upstairs to a smaller, deserted one. There she filled two tall glasses with ice water. She drank hers fast, spilling a tiny drop on her neck. As it rolled down her skin and disappeared into the bodice of her dress, she gave a self-deprecating laugh, color seeping into her face.

I drank from my own glass, the water feeling cool on my tongue, but it did little for the heat rising in my veins as I tried to look everywhere except where the water had fallen.

"Where did *you* learn to dance?" she asked, popping a piece of ice into her mouth.

"Well, basically every Beaumontian prince—or anyone with noble heritage—learns to dance from a very young age, especially the waltz. That's the standard at our gatherings these days, sprinkled with a few variations from those who actually enjoy dancing."

"It's a good thing to learn. Great exercise."

I leaned back against the counter. "Yeah, but when we were teens, it was boring. We'd sneak out of the ballroom, one-by-one, into another room or out into the gardens where we could have our own music and modern dancing."

"So that's why Lucida has all those lights on at the guest house. So the younger kids can take a break with chaperones."

"Smart."

"You know any other dances or just the waltz?"

"A few."

"Good." She gave me a slow smile that made heat stir in my stomach. "Care to try them out?"

I set down my glass and offered my arm. "Absolutely."

When we returned to the ballroom, Damien was climbing onto the stage where the orchestra was playing. "Thank you for coming to celebrate with us tonight," he said, calling everyone to attention. "I want to officially announce my engagement to Amelia Lennox, the most incredible woman in the world."

As people clapped and cheered, Mel joined him on the stage, and Damien continued, "I've been trying to convince her to elope, but for some reason she's sided with everyone who thinks it's a better idea to plan a ceremony for six months." Laughter rippled through the crowd as he repeated his statements in French. "But I'm pleased to announce," he continued, "that I have managed to cut down our engagement time to a torturous three months." More laughter.

Damien took Amelia's hand and stared into her eyes. "Thank you, Miel, for coming into my life and for doing me this honor. I pledge my heart to you." Lowering his head, he kissed her thoroughly, and then signaled the music to start up again.

"Miel?" I whispered to Harper. "I thought everyone called her Mel."

"His nickname for her."

Miel meant honey in French, which might seem a natural

endearment to her, but it wasn't used as much in Beaumont as in America. At least if movies were any indication. "Nice," I said.

"Nice? Are you kidding? That's like saying the sun's temperature is warm. Every woman in here is melting right now."

My laughter came again without effort. "I'll keep that in mind."

We danced a traditional waltz, the Viennese Waltz, and numerous variations we made up on the spot. On the rare occasions when the orchestra played the right music, we also tried the foxtrot, the two-step, and even a moderate version of the swing— the best we could do with the music and all the people in the way. Harper kept up with me beautifully.

"Hey," Harper said during a brief lull, "I think we're beginning to attract attention."

Sure enough, people were staring at us, as though wondering what we planned next. I hadn't felt on display this much since the party my parents threw for my college graduation. And was that my mother talking to the red-faced woman with the very young daughter? Why were they looking my way?

"Maybe we should sit a few out." I offered my arm to lead Harper off the floor. We snagged drinks from a tray before heading to one of the less-crowded sitting rooms off the ballroom.

"So what do you do?" she asked as we sat on a loveseat, sipping the fruity substance. "I mean, besides coming to these things."

"Furniture. My family has a business that makes upscale furniture. Much of what you've seen at the palace—well, the stuff that's not more than a hundred years old—is ours. We have pieces in all the best houses." I patted the loveseat. "This, for instance."

She looked at the loveseat more closely. "Very nice."

"Nice?" I repeated. "Every woman in here melts for my furniture."

She laughed. "You got that right."

Too bad it was for my furniture and not for me. Did she melt for her fiancé? Probably.

"And you?" I asked. "What do you do?"

"I'm an interior designer."

"Ah, so you actually know how good this piece is."

Her fingers caressed the cherry trim. "I do." Her eyes came up slowly to meet mine, and for a moment my breath lodged in my throat. I must be more out of shape than I thought—all that dancing was catching up to me.

My mother appeared in the doorway of the room, skirting around small clumps of people to get to us. "There you are." Her eyes rested on Harper for a moment. "I saw you two dancing. Very nice."

Nice? No, it was melting, I thought, trying to hide my smile. I glanced at Harper and she winked at me.

"It's a pleasure to see dancing like that," my mother said. "Reminds me of when I was young. We all used to dance with a bit more flare in those days."

From her attitude, I could tell she liked Harper—or at least the fact that I seemed interested in her. Apparently, my mother didn't know about the engagement. If I was lucky, maybe she wouldn't force me to attend the luncheons she was probably arranging with her friends tonight, luncheons that would inevitably include their many eligible daughters.

My stomach clenched. She'd been talking to the red-faced woman. Maybe I shouldn't rely on luck alone. Harper was fun and totally out of reach, which meant she was exactly what I needed.

"Mother," I said as the idea formed. "With you and dad living indefinitely at the lake house, I've been thinking maybe you're right about taking the opportunity to update our main residence. It just happens that Harper is an interior designer."

My mother didn't hesitate. "Oh, what a fabulous idea! Would you be interested?" She walked to the other side of our loveseat to perch on a vacant chair near Harper. "Lucida said it was you who updated Damien's main drawing room. It's elegant. Exactly what we need for our house."

My mother looked so eager that she must already be imagining me bouncing little babies on my knees—babies that looked like Harper. That made me feel guilty, but not enough to take back my words.

"What do you say, Harper?" I urged. "Will you come and take a look? See if you can do anything for us?"

Harper stared first at me and then at my mother. "Sure," she said at last. "I would be happy to give you a bid."

"Great!" I might have overdone the enthusiasm.

My mother patted Harper's arm. "We'll talk more later. I'm sure you two have better things to do at this party than to discuss design. Have fun." With another cat-ate-the-canary smile, my mother stood and glided from the room.

The second she was gone, Harper glared at me, her amazing eyes flashing anger. "What do you think you're up to?"

I blinked. "Excuse me?"

"Are you hiring me to work on your house or to pretend to be your girlfriend?"

Chapter 3

Harper

*H*e was so busted. I couldn't believe he'd fake wanting me to update his décor when all he really wanted was to throw women off his scent.

"Look, I get that your mother is pushing you—that's the job of all mothers with adult children—but I have a fiancé, and I don't want him to read about me in the next gossip column about your family, or your . . . your . . . princely exploits."

I expected him to reach down into his never-ending bucket of gentlemanlyness and offer me an apology, but instead he laughed. "Princely exploits? Oh, come on. I promise there will be no articles, and I really do need the house updated—especially if my mother is to entertain there in her efforts to find me a wife. You wouldn't want to delay that, would you? You'd actually be helping her in the long run."

"Riiight," I said. "And you didn't just let your mother think you asked me because you like me."

"I *do* like you. It's not my fault you happen to be engaged." The warmth in his gaze made me want to look away, but I held his stare. "Anyway, we're friends, right? Or becoming friends. And I'll be happy to pay you what you're worth. Please?" He turned up the wattage in the smile. Man, he was fine. More than fine.

Not that it mattered because I was in love with Graham. Completely and totally.

"Unless you're planning to go back to the States soon," he added.

Up until a few weeks ago, I had been planning to return home. There were a million things I needed to do before my wedding, but now with Mel staying here, Emerson delaying the start of his new job, and my mother still traveling, there didn't seem to be any reason to leave Beaumont. Well, except to finish planning the wedding and to pack up my apartment for the years I would be in Germany. Neither of which seemed appealing, especially as I could do what remained of the wedding planning over the Internet or phone.

"I'll be here for a while," I admitted.

"Perfect. Shall I send a car for you tomorrow? Unless you have plans, of course. It's just that it's Saturday and I wasn't going to work, but I can rearrange my schedule next week, if necessary."

The only thing I had planned was sleeping in late and waiting to talk to Graham over the Internet. Yes, my life was chock full of excitement. "How about eleven? I could work it in then."

"Okay, it's a date—deal, I mean. Appointment." Sheepishly, he offered me his hand, and I was glad I was wearing gloves. Even so, my skin tingled at his touch. His chuckle made me worry he'd noticed how quickly I pulled away.

"What?" I said.

"I was thinking about princely exploits. What are you imagining, I wonder?"

I had to join his laughter. "I don't know. Dancing with strange girls, drinking strange concoctions, staying up late in strange places."

"All that, huh? Then I'm guilty as charged—and all of it tonight. Well, I'm not sure Damien would appreciate me calling his house strange." He winked at me. "Must be that new designer he hired."

"Probably." I rolled my eyes as I rose. "Look, I promised my friend I'd dance with him. Thank you for the dancing—and the job offer."

He also arose. "I haven't had so much fun at one of these things in . . ." A shadow brushed over his face, but just that fast it was gone. "Well, it's been a long time. Thank you. I look forward to working with you."

Something in the way he said "working with you" raised my warning indicators. Was that his ploy? To win me over to his fake girlfriend plan by spending time with me? "Just so you know, I usually hire a crew. I don't actually do the work myself."

"Of course. And not to worry; I won't hover. But I thought maybe you'd want to use some of our newest furniture or one of my upholsterers. A tour of my factory might be in order."

For some reason the explanation deflated me. "Good idea," I said.

"I'll walk with you back to the ballroom." He took the empty glass from my hand and deposited both of them on a table near the wall where the servers would soon find them.

The orchestra was playing another waltz, but Emerson wasn't dancing. Instead he was glowering at Stefania, Damien's younger sister, as she whirled around the dance floor with another man. "Good," he said when he saw me. "You've got to get me over there. The guy is totally in love with her. I'm losing ground here."

"Could be," Tristan said not-so-helpfully. "That's one of my cousins, Marcello. He's had a crush on her since grade school."

"No," moaned Emerson, his green gaze falling on me in despair. Then Tristan's words seemed to sink in. "Your cousin? You're a prince too? How many of you are there?"

"Never mind that," I said. "I thought you two were dancing."

Emerson's gaze shifted back to me. "We did for a while at the guest house—that stuff I can figure out. But this . . ." He waved at the dancers. "This, I can't make sense of. I didn't want to keep her from having fun, so I stupidly told her to go dance. And she did!"

"Of course she did. And that *was* stupid."

"I know that now." He ran a hand through his blond hair, making it stand on end. I hadn't seen him this upset over a girl since his freshman year in college when he couldn't get dates because of his horrible acne. Those times were long past, though. Now he was a babe magnet.

"Anyway, we practiced for hours yesterday. You danced fine then."

"I know, but now people are watching."

"So?" I glanced at Tristan, who looked amused but showed the good sense not to laugh. I grabbed Emerson's hand. "Look, I'll dance with you to ease you into it, but you have to remember it isn't how you dance that makes Stefania like you."

"That's right." Tristan patted him on the back. "For instance, you could be a perfectly great dancer, but the girl might be in love with another man."

I turned on him. "You are not helping."

"How about I go dance with Stefania, then?" he said. "That way we can limit my cousin's influence."

Emerson's eyes narrowed. "You'd do that for me?"

"Of course."

"Thanks, man." Emerson shook his hand and let me prod him onto the floor. No sooner had he put his hand on my waist than he leaned in to whisper, "He doesn't have a secret crush on Stefania too, does he?"

"No. He's hiding out from the other women here who are after him. Stefania's much too young for him."

That made Emerson relax, but his fateful expression didn't leave. "Maybe this is all a bad idea. She's going back to England for school, and if I put off my employer in America any longer, I might not have a job."

"Those are problems for another day," I told him. "Tonight we dance. Now remember, *you* are supposed to lead."

At first it was like trying to push around a rock on a sticky surface, but gradually he loosened up and took over the lead. "That's right," I said. "Now don't forget to smile."

"So much to remember," he muttered.

The music stopped and started again, and we continued dancing. True to his word, Tristan had cut in with his cousin, and he and Stefania danced well together, which had me wishing . . . I couldn't finish the thought.

"Okay, I think you're ready," I told Emerson as the second song ended. "Go. Hurry!"

He made a beeline for Stefania, who smiled when he spoke to her. Tristan glanced in my direction and our eyes met and held. I couldn't look away. He started in my direction as a man next to me said, "Would you like to dance?"

The man stepped closer, and I placed him as one of Gabriel's cousins that I'd met at the palace with Mel, but I couldn't remember his name. "Yes. Of course," I said.

He offered me his arm to walk me into the dancers. "Nice to see you again. You look very lovely tonight."

"Thank you. It's a wonderful party."

That pretty much comprised the entirety of our conversation. He was a precise dancer, with absolutely none of the intuition and grace that Tristan had in abundance, or even the raw talent Emerson possessed. At the end of the dance, he escorted me to the edge of the crowd, and there I escaped behind a group of women.

Looking around for Mel, I spotted Tristan instead, dancing with a dark-haired beauty. Neither were talking, and he moved stiffly now, more like his precise cousin than the man who'd dared the two-step here among such reserved company.

Who was she?

Whoever she was, I was guessing they had a past, one he was still conflicted about.

"Oh, Harper," said a voice beside me, "Mel is looking for you."

I turned and looked into the face of Beaumont's new queen. Kami didn't have the same coloring as her sister—Kami had dark hair while Mel was blond—but they looked an awful lot alike.

"Where is she?"

"Over by the orchestra."

"Thanks." I hesitated. "Uh, Kami, who is that woman dancing with Tristan?"

She followed my gaze. "That's Lady Jianne Selmone. They used to date. Everyone thought they'd get married, but it didn't work out. Why the interest?"

"I'm just curious." When Kami waited for more, I added, "He asked me to do some work at his place, so I wanted to know all I could about him. If she's a part of his life, she'd need to be involved."

Kami chuckled. "I don't think you'll have to worry about that." She looked ready to say something more, but instead she clamped her mouth shut and smiled. I knew the queen well enough to understand that whatever she'd wanted to tell me, she wouldn't because she considered it gossip. Well, it didn't matter because I wasn't interested in Tristan's love life. I had my own to worry about.

"Thanks," I said again, and went to find Mel.

She welcomed me with a huge hug and whispered in my ear, "This is the best night of my life! It's just like you said. He looks at me, and my knees go weak, and I can't breathe. Thank you so much for coming with me to Beaumont. I don't know if I would have had the courage to come looking for Kami if you and Emerson hadn't tagged along."

I squeezed her tightly. "Yes, you would have. But, hey, you're my best friend, and you don't owe me a thing. Besides, I had a lot of fun tonight."

"Good. I'm glad."

There wasn't much of the evening left, and as soon as the guests began to say their goodbyes, I excused myself and went upstairs to climb out of my dress and scrub my face clean of makeup. I thought I would fall asleep quickly, but sleep eluded me. Every moment of the night replayed, dancing with Tristan, him kissing my hand, his invitation to redo his house, watching him dance with Stefania and then the dark-haired woman.

I also thought about Graham. The ache of missing him had been so strong when I'd still been at Stanford and he'd first gone overseas. Maybe I was growing used to being alone, or maybe the incident last month had changed things forever. But we had been good together once. Happy. Somehow, I'd make it through these next few months apart—and put his betrayal away in some dark corner where I wouldn't have to look at it too closely.

At last I fell asleep.

I dreamed of dancing.

Harper

"Harper." The voice seemed to come from a million miles away. "Harper?"

I opened my eyes to Mel shaking me. "What? Why are you doing that?"

"Uh, there's someone downstairs waiting for you."

"What are you—" I sat up straight. "Oh, no, no, no, no! I didn't oversleep. It can't be after eleven!"

"Yes, it can." Mel looked amused. "I thought you went to bed early."

"I couldn't sleep." My feet tangled in the covers, and I nearly fell out of bed as I hurried to climb out. "Go down and tell whoever that I'm coming, okay? I need to jump in the shower really quick."

I ran to the closet to choose clothes. What a wonderful way to start my first work meeting with Tristan. He'd be really impressed with me.

"Wait a minute. Where exactly are you going?" Mel followed me inside the closet.

Oh, right. In all the excitement I hadn't told my best friend the details of last night. "Remember Tristan Fontaine? You seemed to know him last night when he came through the reception line. Anyway, I'm going to redo some of the rooms at their family residence."

"I know Tristan. I met him a few times at the palace, and we talked about a new factory he wants to me design for him."

"You never told me."

She shrugged, and the strap of her tank slipped off her shoulder. "How am I supposed to remember which of Gabriel's cousins you've met? I can barely keep them straight myself. I must have met him sometime when you were out with Emerson or talking to Graham. But why did he ask you to redo his house? I mean, how did it come about?"

"Well, at first he was trying to—" I broke off, not really wanting to tell her about him pretending interest in me. It wasn't important. "He was trying to be nice. He likes ballroom dance, and we were practicing a few moves, and suddenly we were talking about me redoing his house with his mother. Apparently, she liked what I did here in the drawing room."

"*Suddenly* you were talking about it?" Mel put her hands on her hips. "Look, you really might want to rethink doing this job."

I paused at the odd tone in her voice, a red blouse in my hand. Red looked great on me, but for some reason orange was the color that really made my skin sing. Except I wasn't trying to impress anyone with my looks, so maybe I needed a more conservative color. "What are you saying?"

"I'm saying that Tristan might be a little hard to work with. That's one of the reason I haven't agreed to help him yet. In fact, it was Kami who warned me, and you know how nice she is to everyone."

"You mean politically correct. That goes along with being a queen." I rehung the red blouse and settled for a royal blue that would go perfectly with my dressy white skort. The blue would enhance my eyes but was conservative enough to be professional.

"But Kami knows his old girlfriend, and the rumor is they split up because he was too controlling. With trying to make this long distance thing work *and* planning your wedding, I don't think you want the headache." She hesitated before adding, "It's not because you need money, is it?" Mel had inherited several lucrative patents from her uncle, after struggling all her life, and she was generous with her money.

"No, it's not that. I thought it would help me pass the time without Graham."

Mel sighed. "When you put it that way, I feel positively lame. Why don't you see how you feel after you talk to Tristan about the job? If you decide to do it, you can set up some ground rules." She smiled. "Besides, I'd like to see him try to push you around."

"That's right. Now go down and stall his driver, okay? I have to shower."

Mel turned on her heel. "Actually, it's not a driver. It's Tristan. Why do you think I'm giving you all this grief?"

This was getting better and better. "Go talk to him about building something then, okay?"

"Okay, but you owe me."

*I*n ten minutes flat I was downstairs, my hair still slightly wet but pinned up in a no-nonsense twist. Mel and Lucida were talking with Tristan in the parlor, but he rose to his feet the minute I entered, my heart pounding from running down the main stairs.

"Good morning," he said, offering his hand. His eyes dipped down the length of me, and I began to worry my skort was too short for a work meeting.

His hand felt warm around mine. "Just barely still morning," I said. "Sorry to keep you waiting."

"I've been in good company." He indicated Mel and Lucida. "Shall we go?"

"Yes. I'm ready."

We left by the front door, where a convertible Maserati in a deep red awaited us. He laughed when he saw my expression. "I know it's cliché, but it's my favorite color. Do you mind the top down?"

My hair would be a mess, but I didn't need to impress him with my looks. "It'd be a sin to put up the top on a day this beautiful."

"Yes, it would. Like dancing the waltz to music meant for a tango."

I jerked my head toward him. "You know the tango?" That was a dance we hadn't tried last night.

"Of course. And I've seen the movies with those scandalous tango scenes. The promise of that dance is the reason we all endured so many lessons."

I laughed. "Right. I can see that."

"But," he added, answering my question, "it really isn't appropriate for a Beaumontian ball, at least not if done properly."

The word *properly* sent a little shiver up my spine. "Especially if one wishes to stay out of the gossip columns."

"Exactly."

The idea of dancing the tango with him was appealing—very appealing. It was my favorite, though it had been years since I'd danced it with anyone but Graham. And how long had it been since I'd danced it even with him? I couldn't remember when.

"Is something wrong?" Tristan asked.

"Oh, no. Not at all." I gave him a smile and pushed thoughts of dancing out of my mind. This was a business relationship. Nothing more. "I thought you were going to send a driver?"

"Yeah, but I ended up not going home last night. I stayed in town. I can't wait for you to see my house. I have to warn you, though, it feels kind of empty since my parents and my brother moved to the lake house, and with my sisters in England."

"How many sisters?"

"Two. Twins. They're in college. My brother is sixteen."

No wonder his parents were anxious for Tristan to marry.

He turned onto the main road, and the car picked up speed. "Main road" was a little bit of an exaggeration since Damien's home was surrounded by acres of olive groves and the primary export of Laval was olive oil.

"What about you?" Tristan asked. "Do you have siblings?"

"I'm an only child, I'm afraid." It wasn't entirely true. I'd had a little brother who'd drowned in our pool when he was only three. To this day, no one knew how he'd gotten through the gate.

We drove for a few moments in silence, and then he said, "It's a bit of a drive, so would you mind stopping for lunch partway?"

"Sure. But how far is it? To your house, I mean."

"All the way north." He glanced at me apologetically. "We have a good two-hour drive."

My jaw dropped. "Oh, I had no idea. I could have driven myself, or taken a taxi. You didn't have to stay over."

"Don't worry about it. I usually drive home after these parties, but I stayed in town not only to give you a lift but because it's better traveling during the day. Besides, driving this car is like going on vacation."

"I'll take your word for it." I wished he'd quit smiling like that because my stomach was doing something funny every time he did.

The car began to slow. "You don't have to take my word." He came to a stop at the side of the road and jumped from the car. "You drive while I call the restaurant."

He didn't have to ask twice. I lifted myself over the gear shift assembly and grabbed the wheel. I knew how to drive a manual transmission, but I'd never driven a Maserati before. I revved the engine a bit too much as I took off, and I glanced at him to see if he minded.

He had his phone in his hands, ready to dial. "You'll get the hang of it. Look, there's the freeway entrance. Take that. But don't go too fast before I finish placing our order, or I'll never be heard over the wind."

"Okay."

I'd always rolled my eyes when guys talked about their motors purring, but this car did purr. It made the blood in my veins sing.

Tristan began talking into the phone in rapid French. I caught the words *bread* and *wine* but nothing more. As soon as he hung up, I punched the gas. The power beneath my feet made me happy the speed limit on this particular stretch was equivalent to eighty miles an hour.

Oh, I love this car, I thought.

Tristan laughed at my expression. "See?"

"Oh, yeah." I was pretty sure most of my hair had escaped its twist, but I didn't care. I could drive like this forever. Off into the sunset where I didn't have to worry about why my fiancé didn't seem to make me a priority. Or why I was so attracted to this prince who was completely off limits.

He's only off limits because you're already taken.

Pushing the traitorous thought aside, I concentrated on the road. The wind blowing through my hair was exhilarating, and I felt like shouting with the thrill running through my body.

"Let me know when you're tired," he said, putting on sunglasses. "We still have a good hour drive before we eat. Or maybe forty minutes at the rate you're driving."

"No way. I'll never be tired of this."

He laughed again.

Chapter 5

Tristan

Watching Harper's delight over the Maserati was like reliving the first time I'd driven my father's convertible as a teen. But then, everything Harper and I did together felt like the first time. The dancing, the flirting. Taking her to my favorite restaurant in the Vallée de la Forêt. With her excitement about driving, I'd also been able to admire the long, lovely length of her legs. I hoped my sunglasses had hidden my fascination.

"So, are you hungry?" I asked as she followed my directions to the restaurant and parked the car.

"Actually, I'm starved. I seem to have forgotten to eat this morning."

"Good. You'll like this."

Her gaze went to the small building in the center of the tiny town, set off the freeway. "La Table du Chef?" she read.

"The Chef's Table. It's a café, really. I know it doesn't look like much, but one of the locals recommended it when I stopped to buy gas, and now I come here every chance I get. That's another reason I wanted to drive home during the day—so they'd be open. They have their own in-house bakery and a pastry chef who I'd hire in a minute to work for me if her husband wasn't a winemaker who won't leave his vineyards." I hopped out of the car. "Come on."

She tossed me the car keys. "Aren't we going to lock up?"

"Not necessary. Being in Forêt is like going back in time a hundred years. Besides, we'll only be a minute."

"I thought we were going to eat."

"Not here. We're just picking up the food." Because The Chef's Table was a dive, dark and old, but the food was to die for.

When we walked into the dim interior, a young woman washing tables dipped her head at us and fled into the kitchen. Moments later, the pastry chef, Viviana, appeared with two large carryout bags.

I kissed the older woman on both cheeks. "Ah, thank you," I said in French. Like everyone else in this tiny town, she didn't know English.

"It's wonderful to see you," Viviana said, giving Harper a thorough once-over.

"This is Harper Thackery," I said before switching back to English. "Harper, meet Viviana. She's the chef I told you about."

"Nice to meet you," Harper said.

"A pleasure," Viviana replied in French, though I was sure she had no idea what Harper had said. Viviana leaned forward to kiss Harper's cheeks in greeting, startling Harper at the familiarity. Unlike in the bigger cities in Beaumont, where people were beginning to lose the custom of kissing, everyone in this town upheld the old traditions. Any friend of mine was a friend of Viviana's, and that meant kissing.

"She's beautiful," Viviana added. "It's about time you brought a woman here."

I pushed a folded wad of bills into Viviana's hand. "It's not like that. She's American, a designer doing work on my house."

Viviana shook her head. "Really? I don't believe it. Your eyes are smiling." To Harper, she said, still speaking in French, "This is a good boy. Don't let him fool you. He likes you."

Harper looked blankly at her, and I chuckled nervously. Even if I was interested, I didn't have a chance. "Thank you for this feast."

"Go now and have fun," Viviana said. "Too much work is bad, even for a prince." More kisses and we were back outside, blinking in the sunlight.

"She seems to like you a lot," Harper said.

"I like her too."

"So where are we going now?"

"You'll see." I drove this time, heading to the north edge of town where a castle stood on a hill. The castle itself was in disrepair, and the grounds overgrown, but several round stone tables lay scattered about the grounds, undamaged and eternal.

"This is like stepping back into time," Harper breathed as I set the bags of food on one of the tables. She started to sit on a stone seat, but I layered it first with a picnic blanket I'd taken from my car. "Better put this down or your white skirt . . . uh, shorts . . . might stain."

"Skort," she said, sitting with a smile that made me wonder if she'd noticed my attention to her legs. "It's just a rock," she mused, "but it's the perfect size. It feels like a stool."

"Been used as a stool for hundreds of years. And these trees are how Forêt was named. It means forest. The full name is Vallée de la Forêt, which more or less means Forest Valley."

"Makes sense." She grimaced as her stomach gave a loud growl. "I guess you heard that."

I laughed. "Mine is doing the same thing. I hope you like *jambon de forêt*." I pulled out one of the sandwiches Viviana had prepared. The *jambon de forêt* wasn't just any ham but one spiced to perfection and smoked, then sliced thin for lunch meat. They made it locally, and like the pastries, it was the best I'd ever had, especially layered on a fresh baguette with lettuce and cheese.

Harper's laugh echoed over the empty clearing. "You come all the way out here for sandwiches?"

"Not just *any* sandwiches. *Viviana's* sandwiches. No one ever thinks to serve me sandwiches."

"I know what you mean. Your bread here is amazing, but I don't think I've eaten one sandwich all summer except when Mel and I go riding. Seriously, it's like everyone is constantly trying to impress us with elaborate dishes."

"That's why I come here." I pulled out my sandwich, unwrapped the paper, and took a large bite. "Mmmm." I swallowed and added, "When we were young, my cousins and I would go camping and this is what we'd bring."

"Camping sounds fun."

"We'd take tents and a boat and go down the river and find a good spot to set up. We'd be gone several weeks all on our own. Well, not Gabriel, obviously. When he or his brother came, so did their bodyguards, but those were simpler times."

"Sounds so normal. Except the bodyguard part." She pulled a piece of ham from her sandwich and ate it. "It is marvelous, I admit. Thank you."

We chatted and talked of her family and mine as we ate our sandwiches, washed down by a glass of Beaumontian wine. Viviana had also included pastries—more than we could ever eat in a single day, but Harper certainly tried.

She scrunched her eyebrows in a way that made something

inside me shift. "I just can't help myself," she admitted. "I've gained five pounds here with all the pastries I've been eating— despite walking for miles every morning."

I couldn't help looking at her figure when she said that, but if there was any extra weight, it had definitely gone to all the right places. Having two sisters, I knew better than to say anything. "That's because you didn't grow up eating them. Give it another few months and you won't crave them so much."

"Really? And how is that working for you with your *jambon* sandwiches?"

I laughed. "That's different."

"Not." She glanced up to where we could still see the towers of the castle poking above the trees. "Can we go up there? To see the castle?"

I was hoping she'd ask. "Sure. They've had to board up some of the old castles in Beaumont because of vandalism, but the court-yards and battlements here are still open."

"Let's go."

Storing the rest of the pastries in one of the food bags, I followed Harper as she wound her way through the overgrown path that angled upward. Finally, we reached the cobblestone drive that would have been used for horses and carriages. As I'd promised, the thick wood door to the courtyard stood open.

Inside the walls, the main courtyard boasted a cobblestone floor, benches under a few scraggly trees, and narrow stairs that led up to the battlements. Hardy weeds languished in the flow-erbeds. The well sitting in the middle of the main courtyard still held clean water, but it had been boarded up for fifty or sixty years. In a second courtyard. we wandered through several open-faced alcoves, which would have been used to shelter the king's small army—and even their animals—during times of trouble.

There was also an open kitchen with a huge fireplace for food preparation, and a separate courtyard with a hard-packed dirt floor for weapons training.

"My ancestors built these castles all over Beaumont to protect the cities from invaders," I explained to Harper. "They haven't been needed for years, of course, and often only those in the larger cities are kept up."

"Who owns them now?" She had taken a small camera from her purse and began snapping pictures.

"The cities usually, but some still belong to different members of my family." I wasn't sure I was ready to share with her the particulars of this castle, especially in light of the disrepair. I hadn't been here in so long.

"What's in there?" She pointed to the thicker section of the castle, which stretched between two of the round turrets.

"Some medieval castles in Beaumont are made up of only walls and battlements," I said. "Others have a keep in the middle where people slept in one or two rooms—with only one entry from a sort of catwalk halfway up the turret that they could easily defend. Others, like this one, had a living section attached. The King of Beaumont lived here at one point in the fourteen hundreds, and that's when most of the living space was added. In fact, for the construction, he used stones that had once made up the outer walls since they weren't needed for defense at that time. Everything of value has since been removed, of course, but it's kept shut to preserve it."

"It's a shame they haven't opened the inside to the public. I mean, for tours."

"Who would come out here?" I shook my head. "There are many other larger and easily accessible castles in Beaumont, one practically for every old city."

She sighed. "Still, it would be nice to see inside. What's the use of protecting it if no one ever enjoys it?"

She had a point. No one except me had seen the interior of this castle for a very long time. Maybe it was time to share. "You really want to go in?"

She nodded. "But I suppose that would be a few hoops to jump through, even for you."

I fished in my pocket and drew out my keys. "Not really."

Her eyes widened. "You have keys?"

I loved surprising her. "This castle and the land here? It was a present to my third great-grandfather on my mother's side when he was given the title Duc de Vallée for being a loyal knight and leader of the king's army—the king at the time happened to be my eighth great-grandfather on my father's side. Duc de Vallée referring to Forest Valley, of course. So my father's ancestors built the castle, but it came down to me through my mother's family line. The castle's been empty for at least the past hundred years. The last Duc de Vallée, my grandfather, married late and had no sons, but he wouldn't pass the castle or title on to my mother."

"Very traditional, huh?"

"Yeah, but not enough to give the dukedom to his nephews as some thought he might. Eventually, my mother married my father, who was the second son of the king of Beaumont—that would be Gabriel's grandfather, and mine, of course—and they had me. My grandfather left the castle to me in his will when I was six, and I received his title when I came of age." I felt slightly embarrassed when I added, "As the son of a king, my father was given another title that's supposed to pass to me when he dies, but I believe I've convinced him to give it to my brother."

"He can choose?"

"If I'm willing. We have an in with the current king."

She laughed. "I see. So that's really why you came to Forêt and found the café and Viviana."

"Well, I did actually need gas too, but yes, I wanted to see my inheritance."

"Okay, then open the door already. Let's see inside."

There was a chain with a padlock, as well as a new lock on the door itself. I opened them both and pulled the heavy door open.

"I never realized castle doorways could be so short," Harper said as she went inside.

My head barely skimmed the stone of the archway. "Only some castles. Smaller doors meant less chance of invaders getting inside, I think. I mean, aside from the fact that many people were shorter back then. I'm not sure why this wasn't enlarged back when they added the living space. If I ever fix it up, I'll enlarge the entry doors and the windows."

"You've thought about redoing it?" She stopped walking, interest apparent in her voice.

I had but never seriously—until this moment. *She's off limits,* I reminded myself. Even if I had been looking for a relationship, she was engaged, and that relationship deserved respect. "Maybe," I said. "Come on. I'll show you around."

There were kitchens, drawing rooms, and other various rooms whose purposes were long since lost to my knowledge. All the furnishings had been removed except a few frayed tapestries that had seen more than their share of mice. Up a flight of narrow stairs were sleeping rooms, sitting rooms, counsel rooms, and what might have been the king's bedroom.

"The whole castle is much larger than I guessed from the outside," Harper said as we investigated a turret.

"I know. Not quite the palaces they began to build later, but nice for that time."

"Nice for any time." Harper rubbed her hands along her bare arms. "But cold."

"Yeah, the older castles were never warm. That's another thing that would have to be added."

The turret's circular staircase went up to a small room that gave us a beautiful view of the surrounding countryside. "Can we get to the walls from here?" Harper asked.

"There's a doorway halfway down the stairs. I have a key." Retracing our steps, we opened the door and went onto the walls. We wandered around the parapets, investigating every interesting turn.

"You can see there is significant erosion in some parts," I pointed out.

"So it's really a matter of total reconstruction, not simple interior design," she mused. "Still, there is so much potential. I mean, if one had the money for it."

"You don't think it would be too lonely for a family to live here?" I had worried about that the one time I'd brought Jianne to see the grounds.

"Well, maybe for a permanent residence."

With that less-than-enthusiastic response, it no longer seemed like a good idea to bring Harper here. I'd never shared this place with anyone besides my immediate family and Jianne. I'd thought since Harper was a visitor who was likely excited about castles and their design, it would be okay, but now I felt—at least a little bit—that I'd exposed too much of my heart. Because I loved this castle, and sometimes I wished I could move in and stay.

"It's getting late," I said, leading us back inside the main keep. "We should probably leave. My mother is planning to meet us at my house to discuss the redesign." The words were true enough, though she wouldn't arrive until dinnertime. I'd told her to come then because I'd wanted to get a feel for what Harper planned before my mother came with her sometimes forceful input.

"All right, but I do think living here would be perfect for weekends or holidays or a summer with family and friends." She laughed as we turned down a corridor. "I mean, it's so peaceful, and with pastries and amazing ham sandwiches close by, what else do you need?"

What else indeed? Maybe she did understand why I thought this place was special.

"Wait . . . look." Harper's voice was scarcely a breath. "Is this some kind of ballroom? Would they have had them back then?"

"It's the great hall," I said, following her inside the spacious room. " At least that's what the raised dais seems to indicate."

I tried to imagine what it might have looked like back in the day, but now that Harper had named it a ballroom, I could only imagine a roaring fire in the huge hearth and people dancing. Aside from a heavy layer of dust and black stains on the walls where torches had once burned, it looked amazingly intact. I studied the arched ceiling to be sure it was still as secure as when I'd had a construction team look at it a few years ago to prevent further disrepair. It looked safe.

Harper walked into the middle of the room and bowed low in a deep curtsey to an invisible partner before beginning a traditional waltz. I watched her swing and twirl for a good minute before I couldn't stand it anymore and joined her, dancing in tune to music we heard only in our heads.

I leaned close to whisper, "We've gone quite crazy, haven't we?"

"Not yet," she said. "This isn't the tango, after all."

She was staring up at me, her ebony hair glistening in the darkness, her eyes alive, her lips parted. Some of her hair had escaped its prison on the drive, softening her face and making me wonder what it would look like completely down. How the strands would feel against my fingers.

My feet stopped moving. Before I realized what I was doing, I was lowering my head toward her. Closer. Closer. My heart thundered a beat that had nothing to do with any waltz. I could almost taste the softness of her lips. Only a few more inches.

With a little gasp, she stepped back, saving us both. "We really should be going. Wouldn't want your mother to wait." She walked toward the door. "Problem is, I'm a little turned around."

"Come on. I'll show you out." I resumed our initial path through the castle, internally berating myself. Some gentleman I turned out to be, trying to kiss a woman promised to another man. What was wrong with me? Harper was meant to be a distraction, a way to buy myself more time before I stepped up for my duty. That's all.

Duty. I clenched my fists.

For the first time in my life, I wished I wasn't the elder brother, a duke, or a prince. That I had met Harper at another time and place. Before her fiancé.

Outside, the sun hung noticeably lower in the sky, signaling that more time had passed than I'd thought. I busied myself with the padlock, wondering how I could undo the damage with Harper. The tension between us was so thick I could barely breathe.

Part of me agonized over how I could make her trust me again. The other part of me, the more vocal part, wished I hadn't stopped before finishing the kiss.

Harper

Had I imagined the almost kiss? Out in the bright sunlight, it seemed so. But Tristan was avoiding my gaze, so maybe I hadn't. *It was just the moment,* I thought. The romance of being in an abandoned castle, of imagining what it had been like all those years ago. Or what it could be again. My fingers itched to explore and sketch and redesign.

But that wasn't the job I'd been asked to do.

As we started down the cobbled drive toward the car, Tristan walked straight ahead, presumably to follow the narrow road that would lead to where we'd parked the car. Instead, I veered off to the left, heading to the trails that led into the trees.

"Where are you going?" he asked.

I stopped and put my hands on my hips. "Did you forget the rest of the pastries? No way am I leaving them for the squirrels. All that walking around has made me hungry."

We both laughed, and the tension between us vanished. "Me too." He angled in my direction, and we retraced our steps to the remains of our lunch. "Thanks for reminding me," he said.

I'd known he'd forgotten, exactly as I'd known he'd join my dance in the castle. That almost kiss—that mistake—was every bit as much my fault as his. What was I doing here with him? If I couldn't keep this professional, I'd have to refuse the job.

Maybe I should anyway.

We ate pastries on our way to the car, where he offered to let me drive again. I shook my head, pushing on my sunglasses. "I think I'll look at the countryside this time."

Which I did for a good ten minutes until the fullness of my stomach and the warmth of the sun won out over the racing wind, and I started to doze. Before I knew it, the car was stopped and a hand landed on my shoulder.

"Harper, we're here."

I opened my eyes, my head turning to the mansion on my right. No, not a mansion, but a palace with dozens of rooms. "Wow," I said. "It's incredible."

"I know it resembles the Beaumontian palace, since it was built by the same man. This was what you might call a country house for the royal family hundreds of years ago, but it was gifted to my father when he married, as he was second in line for the thone at that time. It's actually only a third of the size of the royal palace, and there are notable differences in design."

"Oh, yes, it's definitely unique."

He walked around to open my door before leading me under an archway, past elaborate flowerbeds and statues, to double doors that opened before we reached them. "We passed a gate on the drive up," he explained. "They're expecting us."

I was unsure who "they" were, but an older man with graying

hair waited in the doorway. He dipped his head toward us and spoke as we entered, his Beaumontian-flavored French sounding more Beaumontian than I was accustomed to hearing. He said something I thought might be "welcome home" and something more about the car.

Tristan answered him in rapid French before introducing him as Barbier, the butler. The old man and I both did a lot of nodding and smiling.

"Barbier's a nice man," Tristan said as we left the butler at the door. "Hard working, too. Been with my family for years. I told my mother I don't really need anyone to answer the door anymore—I mean in this day and age—but that's only one of his duties, and he insists on doing it, so I let him."

We'd reached the end of the hallway, and he stopped. "Um, before we take the tour, would you like to freshen up?"

I looked down at myself. "No, I'm fi—oh, maybe I do." My skort was miraculously still white after our excursion in the dusty castle, but my knees had not fared as well. I also needed to use the restroom. "Thank you."

"There's a guest lavatory—uh, bathroom here," he said, pointing down another hallway. "Take your time. I'll meet you in the front drawing room afterwards."

"And where is that?"

He grinned. "Sorry. I forgot, you're—of course you don't know. It was the room on the right when we entered. Just off this main hall."

Main hall. As opposed to the semi-main hall or the secondary hall or the minor hall that was probably located on some remote floor? I found myself smiling as I entered the guest bathroom. The décor was nearly perfect in red and gold, with intricate molding that sent me back to another time. The only things I didn't like were the wide mirror over the two sinks, the inadequate lighting, and a wall that had nothing but a small picture to break up the solid expanse of red. Easy fixes.

Soft gold hand towels made short work of the dirt on my legs and feet that I shamelessly washed in the bidet. I didn't think many visitors would be using the bidet for cleansing other bodily parts, but the staff would probably sterilize it anyway long before another guest stepped foot inside the room. I cleaned off the tops of my sandals and folded the dirty towels over the bidet itself so the staff would know it had been used.

Next, I faced the tangled mess of my hair. I was glad I'd brought a brush because I really didn't want to meet Tristan's mother looking so wind-blown. There was a soft couch in a room adjoining the bathroom, and for a moment I was tempted to lie down and rest. Instead, I went back to the sink and splashed water on my face.

When I entered the drawing room, Tristan was waiting, his dark hair slightly damp as if he'd tried to tame it after our drive. I liked it better the other way and felt a compulsion to reach up and tousle it.

"Something funny?" he asked.

I really needed to learn not to show my emotions on my face. Instead of answering his question, I began roaming the room. The furniture was elegant, though some was extremely dated and might be better in a museum. The room was overly crowded, as if the family had collected more and more possessions over the years and couldn't bear to remove anything. As a result, there was a clash of styles and the large space seemed cramped.

My mind was already churning, seeing the drawing room as it could be. "Is this one of the rooms you want me to redo?" I asked. The wallpaper here was yellow and definitely needed to go if it was to be a real family home and not a museum.

"If you think it needs anything." He surveyed the room doubtfully.

"Oh, it does. Believe me."

He frowned. "This is actually one of my favorite rooms. I thought it might not need much updating."

"It'll be much better. I promise you. Now show me everything else. Unless you want to wait for your mother."

"No, that's okay. I'd like to hear what you think before she arrives."

From the drawing room we went to the dining room, the music room, the gentlemen's drawing room, the ladies' drawing room, the children's drawing room, the huge kitchens, Tristan's office, a library, and more. Every room revealed the same problem as the front drawing room. They didn't need so much a redesign as a declutter and reorganization. Except for that awful yellow wallpaper in the front drawing room, which definitely had to go.

The last room on the main floor was the ballroom. I caught my breath as we entered, my gaze going to the beautiful crystal chandeliers. The layout was perfect, though much too dark with the same red and gold that had been in the bathroom. "What a wonderful room," I murmured.

"It has nice lines," Tristan agreed. "But I was thinking something more in a navy blue."

I stared at him. "No. Just no."

He blinked, his eyebrows shooting up and his jaw firming. "And what is wrong with blue?"

"Nothing's wrong with blue. It's just all wrong for this ballroom. What we need is to alleviate the red with some fancy wallpaper and tapestries to keep the elegant feel, and then highlight with dramatic lighting. Throw in some unusual seating and something to set off the orchestra area, and voilá."

"I was really set on blue."

I stood my ground. No way was he going to ruin this ball-room on my watch. "Blue I can do in your office. But this place is too great to ruin it with a color change."

He looked ready to protest further, but I shook my head, preempting the objection. "I'll do a mockup for you. Show you what it will look like. I have a computer program on my laptop back at Damien's. You need to trust me on this." Stepping away from him, I drew out my phone and began taking pictures.

When I glanced back at him, there was an odd smile on his face, and I wondered if anyone had ever told him he was wrong. Well, he'd better get used to it. Being a prince didn't mean he knew about design. I might not have lived in Beaumont all my life, but I hadn't spent the past four months sitting on my thumbs. I'd learned more by attending parties and studying exquisite Beaumontian houses than I'd learned in four years of traditional schooling.

I gave him my best smile. "Are there any other rooms?"

"Well, the upstairs should be looked at, and the guest house, but those rooms can wait until the main floor is finished. Why don't we go outside and have some tea? After all this walking around, I bet you're hungry." A smile danced on his lips. Was he implying something with that comment? Well, I didn't care. At least I wouldn't starve working for him.

"I'd love to."

He led me outside to a large patio, where a pool glistened in the late afternoon sun. I was vaguely aware of trees and manicured flowerbeds, but the water filled my perception, beckoning with a siren's call that was only in my head. "Is something wrong?" he asked, settling into a padded bronze chair next to a table.

"No." I forced my eyes away from the water.

As if on cue, a woman in a pink dress and a huge white apron appeared with a tray of iced tea and an array of cookies and biscuits. I'd grown used to the custom of having tea at Damien's, but the iced tea was different.

Tristan noted my interest. "You don't like it? I should have asked. I can have Carmen get something else."

"No, this is fine. I don't think I've ever had iced tea in Beaumont before." Was his not asking a sign of exerting control? I shook my head to dispel the thought. What did it matter? It wasn't like I was dating him.

"It's definitely not traditional," he explained, "but it's a summer custom for my family."

My eyes wandered back to the water, moving now under the merest breeze.

"You can stay here during the remodel," Tristan offered. "I could arrange for a place in town, but that seems pointless when I have more than enough space and you'll have to spend so much time here anyway. My secretary will connect you with the right people to get the work done. Will that be all right?"

I hadn't considered the need to be close. Obviously, I couldn't stay with Mel at Damien's or even with Kami. Too much time would be wasted in the commute. Yes, staying here would be the most convenient. So why did I feel so reluctant?

Tristan was watching me, his eyes bottomless. Vividly, I remembered what it was like to have his arms around me during our dances. No, staying here was definitely not a good idea. I'd have to stay in town.

"I won't be here much of the time, of course," he added. "I generally keep late hours at work."

"I see." That would be different then. "I'll have to get my laptop and my clothes."

"If you'd rather not take the long drive back, I can send someone for your things in the morning."

"But I didn't bring anything with me for tonight."

"I have two sisters your size," he said, "and closets full of clothes. Believe me, finding something to sleep in will be the least of your problems."

I laughed in spite of myself because as beautiful as the country-side was, I hadn't been looking forward to driving home tonight. "Okay, you convinced me. I'll call Mel. She'll know what I need."

I reached for my phone. "Excuse me for a moment," I said. So much to tell her, but not with Tristan listening in. Standing, I walked the length of the pool, feeling slightly dizzy with the move-ment of the water. *Don't look at it,* I told myself. But I couldn't tear my gaze away.

Mel picked up on the first ring as if she'd been waiting for me. "So, how's it going?"

"This place is amazing," I said. "And did you know Tristan also owns a real live castle in a little town off the freeway? Anyway, I'm going to make up the designs and give him a bid." I glanced over to wear Tristan was sitting, looking over the gardens. "I don't know if he'll accept it because he has some weird ideas about color, and life is too short to work on projects I can't be proud of, but I think he'll come around. I'll need to stay here for a few weeks, though. Maybe I can come back on the weekends to see you and Emerson. Can you pack up my clothes and my laptop? Tristan will send someone for them in the morning."

"Are you sure about this?" Mel sounded worried.

"I'm sure. Look, it really won't take long. I'll hire a local crew and start working right away. Mostly it's going to mean reorga-nizing and decluttering. This house is huge, but I've never seen so much crammed into any space."

Mel laughed at that. "Yeah, and I know how you feel about hoarding. Hopefully, Tristan will be okay with you junking his old stuff."

"Not junking—storing. Anyway, half of it should be in a

museum. Or at his castle." Hmm, the idea was interesting, but Tristan hadn't hired me for the castle.

"Look, don't worry about sending someone," Mel said. "I'll send one of Damien's people, or maybe Emerson. Stefania decided to leave for England tomorrow instead of Monday, and he needs a distraction."

I laughed. "All right. Let me know."

"Oh, and Harper. Be careful."

"What's to be careful about? It's a job."

Silence and then, "Okay, I didn't tell you this morning, but I did see you two dancing last night . . . and it worries me."

"Because he's a good dancer?"

"No." Another lengthy pause. "Because you looked so happy. You haven't been that way for a while."

I took a deep breath and held it. I'd wanted to tell Mel about Graham's infidelity for weeks now, but he'd confessed and I'd decided to stay with him. End of story. Real forgiving meant all the way forgiving, not airing his shameful secret—even to my best friend. Most of all, I didn't want our future together colored by her anger. Now I wished I'd told her. She'd understand then why I'd been so happy dancing and not thinking about Graham.

"Well, you know how I love to dance," I said.

"Yeah, I know, but it seemed . . . never mind. I know you love Graham. I just don't want to see you hurt."

Mel was sweet, and I refused to be angry with her meddling. "You don't have to worry about that. I promise."

"Good. I'll call you tomorrow."

"Okay." I hung up, pondering the conversation. What was up with Mel? It wasn't as if I'd been unfaithful to Graham. Had I? I'd thought I was only being friendly.

Was this how Graham's relationship had begun with that female soldier? The idea made me feel ill.

The next time I talked with Graham, I'd tell him everything, though I wasn't sure there was anything to tell—or at least nothing I could explain over Skype.

One lesson I'd learned well these past months: long distance romances weren't romantic at all.

Harper

I walked back and sat next to Tristan, aware of his gaze as intently as I was aware of the shimmering water. "All set?" he asked.

"Yes, but she'll send someone with my things in the morning. No need to have your people go."

"Great. Then after we finish our tea, we'll find something for you to wear until then." He followed my gaze to the water. "I'm sure there are swimming costumes if you'd like to swim."

"Thanks." No way would I need one.

"Is something funny? You're smiling."

It was smile or cry, and I didn't need to cry in front of him. Not about a stupid pool. "Just your choice of words. You sounded so British just then. Or Beaumontian. We say swimming suit or swimsuit in America."

He chuckled. "Too bad. Costumes sounds so much more fun."

I set down my glass of iced tea. "Do you have a storage place for furniture we will no longer need on the main floor?"

"No longer need?" He blinked in surprise.

"Look, I don't know how much you have to do with furniture design at your company—"

"Not much, actually."

"—but your biggest problem here is overcrowding and styles that are centuries apart. I'll need someplace to store the pieces we won't need. I'm assuming you'll want to keep them for posterity. Or to donate to a museum."

"Are you sure that—"

"I'll show you in my mockups."

"All right." In a swift movement that reminded me of dancing, he came to his feet and extended a hand to help me up. "I'll show you the storage room."

He took me up the stairs to the third floor, where a room every bit as large as the ballroom was half filled with cloth-covered furniture. Excitement bubbled inside me at the treasure. "Amazing. Is all this from your own factories?"

"Some. Others predate it by decades or more."

I peeked under some of the sheets, already mixing and matching pieces in my head with those down below. He was right that some of the pieces were much older. *Those should go in the castle,* I thought.

He gave me a strange look. "They would look nice there."

Had I actually spoken aloud?

"I mean, if I ever decide to . . ." He shook his head. "It's not likely I'll have the time to live there. I'm afraid that castle will remain closed." Regret laced his voice.

I took out my camera. "Do you have a notebook? I'd like to get started cataloguing. I need to know what I can use so I can work it into the bid."

His hand closed over mine, his warmth seeping through me. "Tomorrow will be soon enough. For now, let's go find you something to wear. I'll have the housekeeper bring up toiletries, of course."

I laughed a little too loudly. "I think that is the first time I've ever heard the word toiletries in actual conversation."

He dropped my hand. "Make fun of my English all you want, but I can't wait to hear you speaking French." It sounded like a promise.

"Now that *would* be funny. Believe me, I've already embarrassed Damien and Mel numerous times, despite the tutor they found for me. Unfortunately, I won't be here long enough to learn."

He sobered instantly, and his eyes became unreadable. "Ah, that's right. You'll be married soon. And then where will you live?"

"Germany for two years, then back to the States. My fiancé's in military intelligence."

"Sounds interesting. I've been to Germany a handful of times, and it's a nice country." His smile finally returned. "Though not nearly as beautiful as Beaumont."

His gaze rested on me in such a way that I felt as if he had called *me* beautiful. My heart thumped loudly, and for a moment neither of us spoke. It should have been awkward, this staring contest, but I could have stood there forever.

He broke the connection first, his eyes going to my skort. "I'm afraid this storage room has succeeded in doing what my castle failed to do."

Looking down, I saw the streak of dust across my white skort. I was about to brush it off but realized my hands were even dirtier.

"Better wash up." He led me from the room and down a flight of stairs to a bedroom suite that was more elegant than the one I used at Damien's but that suffered from the same cluttering as the rest of the house. The sitting room held one too many couches, and the attached bedroom had far too many chairs.

"You can use this suite during your stay here," Tristan called to me as I washed up in the adjoining bathroom. "It belonged to the oldest of my two sisters—and I say that as a joke, since they're twins—before she moved to my grandmother's old room. Identical twins run in the royal family, you know."

I did know because Gabriel was a twin, but as his brother was currently in France with his new wife, I hadn't met him yet.

"Anyway," Tristan continued, "we have other guest rooms, but this is the closest to the stairs and the most comfortable temperature-wise in the summer."

"This will be perfect," I stuck my head out the door to say. Back inside the bathroom, I grabbed one of the dry hand towels and rubbed vigorously at my skort. The dust came off almost completely, leaving only a faint streak that you'd have to examine very closely to see.

I emerged to find him in a dressing room directly off the suite's main sitting room. The dressing room held several couches and a mirror wide enough for five women standing side by side in ball gowns. Smaller connecting doors opened to reveal two walk-in closets, one of which was full of clothes.

"Use anything here you'd like." Tristan pulled a red dress from the closet. "You could wear this for dinner tonight. It would look nice on you." He hesitated and added, "My mother has a feast planned, I believe. That is, if you're up to it."

Maybe that explained why she hadn't arrived yet. I studied the clothes and took out a simple orange pantsuit. "This is really more my color."

He glanced regretfully at the red dress, which almost made me laugh. Red might be his favorite, but it wasn't mine, and if I had to borrow clothes, I wouldn't choose red.

If. Because I didn't need anything. I put the pantsuit back.

"Really, I'd feel uncomfortable borrowing anything." If needed, I could sleep in my blouse and underwear. It might be different if his sister were here to offer the clothes herself, but some of the items still had tags on them, and she could be saving them for a special occasion.

He smiled and said with a flourish of his hand, "As you wish."

"Princess Bride? Really?" Of all the movies he could quote, I hadn't expected that one.

"I have a copy we can watch."

I followed him out of the room, laughing. "*You* want to watch Princess Bride?" I hadn't seen Princess Bride in a year, though in our first few years of college, Mel and I had watched it at least once a month with the other girls in our apartment building.

"It's a funny movie," he insisted. "And the theater is the best room in the house. I had it put in when—" He stopped short, his eyes going to something beyond me. His color didn't so much fade as it leaked from his face.

I turned and saw his mother, Princess Rosina, and the dark-haired woman Tristan had been dancing with at the ball. His ex-girlfriend. Up close, I could see she was around my age, but she possessed the kind of beauty that caused men to go to war. Ironically, she wore a red dress that flattered her curves perfectly, though Tristan's eyes didn't leave her face.

"Jianne," he said. "I didn't know you were coming."

"Your mother invited me for dinner. I hope that is all right." Her English was not as good as his, but better than most.

Rosina smiled at me. "Lady Jianne Selmone is family friend, and I know she has an interest in design, so I decided to stop by on the way here and see if she wanted to come along. I'm sure she'll love hearing your plans."

Somehow I doubted the timing was a coincidence, but I smiled and nodded, wondering why Jianne was really here.

Rosina turned to Jianne. "This, of course, is Harper, the designer I was telling you about."

"Nice to meet you." Jianne didn't smile, and her eyes slid past me without really making contact.

Rosina appeared not to notice. "I trust my son has shown you the house? What do you say—can you help us?"

"Yes, absolutely." Why did I feel like I'd stepped into the middle of a family squabble? Next to me, Tristan was so tense I wondered if he might explode. Was he still in love with this woman who had broken up with him? I was guessing yes.

A wave of disappointment shuddered through me, though I couldn't pinpoint why. His feelings for her shouldn't matter in the least. I wasn't the kind of woman to lead a man on, and I'd been very clear with him about my feelings for Graham and my plans for the future.

Maybe it was myself I hadn't convinced. The thought was disturbing.

"Is everything all right?" Tristan asked, apparently having recovered from his surprise. He was now watching my face, and his hand on my elbow gave me strength.

"Yes, fine. Thanks."

"I would love to hear a bit of what you have planned for the house," Rosina said.

"I can share with you my first impressions." I would have stepped toward her, but I didn't want to leave Tristan's supporting hand. "But it will take me another day or two to really dig into it and come up with an actual bid."

"Of course. I'm sure it'll be wonderful." Rosina motioned to me. "There is still time before dinner. Shall we?"

I stepped away from Tristan and went with her. We wandered

back through the house, Rosina and me in the front, with Tristan and Jianne trailing behind. Every now and then, I could hear them murmuring in French, and I wondered what they were saying. They didn't seem intimate—in fact, a person could walk between them quite comfortably with all the distance they kept.

I explained to Rosina that my focus would be to reorganize and to make better use of the spacious rooms. "Doing so will make the entire place lighter, more inviting."

"Perfect for entertaining," Rosina said with a smile as we left the drawing room. "Tristan has been putting off his obligations far too long." Her gaze went not to Tristan but to Jianne.

"And Tristan is okay with all of these suggestions?" Jianne said in her first comment addressed to me. For someone with an "interest" in design, she had been completely absent from my conversation with Rosina.

"Well, I haven't seen them all yet," Tristan answered. "But so far she has me convinced."

I was glad for that, at least—and that he didn't bring up his suggestion of blue for the ballroom. Jianne nodded and fell silent.

"I'll give you a complete computer rendition before any work begins," I reminded them. "It won't be perfect, but it'll give you a good idea of how it will look."

Rosina waved that aside. "Looking forward to seeing them. I'm sure they'll be perfect. But now it's time for dinner, if everyone is ready?"

She glanced at my skort, as if only now noticing it, though I'd already caught her staring a few other times. Not only had I become convinced she could see the faint dust mark across the front, but she probably thought I was showing too much skin. "We can wait while you change, dear," she added.

I didn't need another prompt. Rejecting Tristan's offer of clothes had mostly been about me showing I couldn't be controlled, but obviously, their family tradition was to dress up when guests came for dinner. Especially guests like Lady Jianne.

It would be nothing to run upstairs, maybe put on the red dress to match Jianne's. No, I wanted to feel confident, which meant the orange pantsuit would be better for me. The pants would assert my autonomy and also make my skin look glowing and healthy. Not that I was trying to compete.

I felt Tristan's eyes on my face, and I looked up to meet his gaze. "I think Harper looks great as she is," he said. "Besides, she didn't bring a change. Now that she's going to do the house, she'll be staying here, but her things haven't arrived yet."

"The girls have left plenty of—" Rosina began. Tristan shook his head and Rosina fell silent. Then she added, "You do look lovely, Harper."

"Thank you. I'll think I'll wash up in my room."

Leaving them all behind, I escaped upstairs, wishing that instead of dinner, I could find Tristan's theater room and bury myself in a movie.

Tristan

"Harper is staying here?" my mother asked. Jianne's eyes fixed on my face. I could feel her wanting to know the answer too, as if she still had a personal stake in my response.

"Of course," I said. "She'll need to personally supervise the work. And there's plenty of room. She can't stay at Damien's and drive four hours each day."

My mother nodded. "She's also perfectly welcome at my house."

"Thanks," I said with finality. "I will let you know if that becomes necessary."

Jianne looked away. "I'd better wash up too." She took one step before stopping and meeting my gaze. "I'd like to talk with you later, if that's okay."

My heart should have been soaring to hear those words, not because of a possible relationship between us, but because of the progress the words signaled she was making at controlling her own destiny. Instead of feeling happy for her, anxiety clawed through me as I wondered if I'd have to hurt her to avoid replaying the events of the past. Even if she was different, something inside me had changed over the year since our breakup, and I didn't want a repeat.

"Of course we can talk," I said. "I'm assuming that's why you came."

"Yes, it is." She darted a look at my mother, and I realized Jianne had not wanted to come tonight, but my mother had insisted.

I waited until Jianne was gone to confront my mother. "Why did you bring her? What were you thinking?"

"I'm thinking of your happiness. I know you still have feelings for Jianne. She broke up with you, but I thought enough time had passed, and you know she showed an interest in redesigning the rooms when you were dating. I thought it was the perfect opportunity to show her what she's lost. Or maybe you could finally come to terms with what happened between you and move on."

"You shouldn't have brought her." Harshness tinged my voice, a harshness I usually never showed to my mother. I struggled to calm my emotions. Whatever she'd done, I knew it was out of love. "It's not going to fix anything."

"Why not? I can tell she still has feelings for you. Can't you forgive her for breaking up with you?"

I couldn't tell her. I'd kept the secret too long: it had been my fault the relationship hadn't worked out. Not Jianne's. I had been the one who ended it.

"Is it because of how you feel about Harper?"

I seized on that. "She's different from anyone I've ever met. I want to get to know her better."

I also wanted to tell my mother how I'd pushed Harper about

using blue in the ballroom and how she'd calmly stuck to her opinion. How she'd firmly told me she liked wearing orange and not red. I'd been impressed by her confidence as she explained her ideas to my mother, who I could tell was doubtful about removing so much of the furniture. Harper had met her head on with boldness that didn't mince words. In fact, the only time I'd seen Harper waver was when my mother wanted her to change for dinner. Which was why I'd stepped in—mostly because Jianne had always needed that interference but at least partially because I really liked the way Harper looked in that white skort. But of course I couldn't tell my mother any of this because that would require explaining to her why I'd broken up with Jianne in the first place.

Several seconds passed as my mother studied my face. My mother who could always tell if I was lying. "Oh, son. I hate to be the one to tell you—Harper's engaged. Lucida told me, but you surely had to notice her engagement ring."

Oh, right. Even if my mother hadn't ferreted out the information, Harper wasn't wearing gloves tonight. So much for letting everyone think we were dating. At least now I understood that bringing Jianne here was more about pushing Harper away than getting Jianne and me back together.

"I know," I said. "But she's not married yet." Before my mother could protest, I raised a hand. "Don't worry. I understand that an engagement is a serious commitment. I don't take that lightly."

"I was only going to add that I was engaged to someone else before your father. Did you know that?"

"I remember the story. But you never told me what convinced you to break it off."

She tapped her hand against my arm. "No, and you don't need to know." Her smile seemed to radiate from her eyes. "Just show her who you really are. I do like her confidence, and her plans for the house, although I'm still not quite sure all that furniture in the drawing room has to go."

"It's going, Mom. I'm giving her a chance."

"All right. You're living here, after all. Now I'm going to see how Carmen is coming along with dinner."

The tenseness in my stomach relaxed. "I hope we're having fish."

"Of course we are."

She passed Jianne coming from the restroom. "You and Tristan go on into the dining room," my mother said. "I'll be right there."

Jianne waited until I reached her to say, "Coming here wasn't my idea. Your mother seemed to think—"

"I know how she can be, but has something changed?"

She looked away. Getting information from her was often like fishing—trying to catch hold of any little thing, then reeling in with all my strength.

As if she was afraid to give me even a glimpse of her true feelings.

I took a breath and probed deeper, because otherwise I'd never know why she was here. "Jianne, has anything changed? Have you been seeing your therapist?"

"Yes, I've been seeing him. Of course I have. I know it makes you happy."

"Ah, Jianne." I took both her hands in mine. "I want you to do what makes *you* happy. That's what you never understood. And that's what seeing your therapist should be about—learning what makes you happy. You shouldn't go because of me."

"I know." Her gaze hovered demurely in the area of my chest. When I'd first met her, I'd thought it was shyness or modesty, and she'd intrigued me. Later, I'd thought I could help her. Now, watching her was like looking at a child—a child in a woman's body. Too afraid to live alone or have opinions of her own, a result of a life with her controlling father. She was away from him now and living with her aunt, but while we were dating, her deference and her fear of doing something that might displease me—or anyone else—had killed all chance of romantic love between us.

I hadn't been able to fix her, not at first with my love or later with doctors. While our match was seen as a good one in society circles, and I'd been attracted to her in the beginning, I couldn't ask her to marry me. I'd barely dared to kiss her, afraid I would be forcing myself on her, that she'd never refuse even if it wasn't what she wanted.

If I had proposed, it would only have been out of a sense of duty, and I had a greater duty to my future children. They needed a mother who was strong, who would fight for them, for herself . . . and for me.

"You like her, don't you?" Jianne said softly.

"What?"

"Harper."

Harper was everything Jianne wasn't. She was strong and knew what she wanted. Unfortunately, what she wanted wasn't me. "Yes, I do."

Jianne stared at the carpet runner lining the hallway. "I wish I were more like her."

"You can be anything you want."

"Too late for us, though?"

The question alone showed it was too late. If she had protested, if she had started fighting for me, if she began expressing her opinions, then maybe there would be a chance. Or maybe if I'd been more patient, kinder, less forceful, I could have given her the confidence she needed. But a year hadn't changed anything, at least not between us. My feelings for Jianne now were protective, like a big brother felt toward a younger sister who had been abused.

"I will always be your friend, Jianne."

For once, she held my gaze. "You saved my life—saved me from my father. I owe you so much."

Before I could protest, she added something that made me hope for her future, because a year before she would never have dared to say it: "I think she likes you too."

Harper

I reapplied my lipstick and tidied my hair again. I thought about scrubbing out the dust a little more from my skort, but Tristan's words of support made me realize that it really didn't matter. Rosina might not admire my dinner outfit, but she seemed to appreciate most of my design suggestions. I was sure they'd love what I had in mind, and I itched to get started making my lists and 3D renditions of my ideas. However, those would have to wait until my laptop arrived.

Taking a deep breath, I marched myself to the door, but my resolve was broken by the ringing of my cell phone. Probably Mel checking up on me. No, it was Graham, and he wasn't calling through the phone but through Skype. I was logged in to Tristan's guest wi-fi already, so after a moment's hesitation, I punched the accept button. The Fontaines would have to wait.

"Hey," I said as Graham's image came into view. His blond

hair was super short, so it didn't have any of the curls I'd admired when we first met. The hair, his pale face, and his army fatigues were the only details I could make out on my small screen.

"Hi honey. How are you?" He was tipping back on his chair in what looked like the mess room, his feet up on a table. He didn't always look so relaxed, especially after they'd been working on a particularly challenging project.

"I'm good. How are you?" My question was as casual as his had been. I didn't worry about him being in danger because most of what he did involved studying aerial photographs of places they were keeping an eye on in the middle east. Sometimes it was taxing emotionally—lives depended on him and his team deciphering what the photographs told them about the enemy—but he wasn't in physical danger. He liked to joke that the safety of being in intelligence was the reason he'd finished college. They had too much invested in him to send him to the front lines.

"I'm great," he said. "You're on your phone? Are you out with Mel?"

"No, I'm at Tristan Fontaine's s—he's a cousin of the king. I met him last night at the party. He's hiring me to redesign his house, so I'll be staying here for a while to get it done. But I'll have my computer again tomorrow." We didn't talk over Skype each day as we had in the beginning, but we always exchanged at least an email.

A commotion somewhere off screen drew his attention, and he leaned forward abruptly, his face taking up the entire screen. "Look, I'm sorry about not being at the party. I really couldn't pass up the opportunity to connect with the officers here."

"I thought you had to work."

"It *was* work. I could have opted out, but it wouldn't have been good for my career. I got the pictures Mel sent. You looked beautiful. Was Emerson able to dance at all?"

"Some. He wasn't half bad."

"I'm glad he was there so you didn't have to sit out."

Should I tell him about Tristan? "Oh, I danced quite a bit. And not just with Emerson. You know me. When will you have leave again?"

"Well, I sort of lost my chance, and everything's scheduled out for the next month. I'm sorry."

Anger waved through me, and I thought about saying I was furious with him for putting non-required work in front of me, especially after Damien had arranged for a private flight. But since Graham's confession last month about his drunken indiscretion with a female soldier—who had supposedly transferred out shortly after—things were different between us. We couldn't talk like we used to. I'd forgiven Graham because of what we had built over the years and because I knew he was sorry, but a little piece of me had died that day. What I needed right now was for Graham to wrap me in his arms, to say that he wanted me and only me. To remind me we were worth fighting for.

"Is something wrong?" he asked.

My gaze drifted back to the screen. Everything was wrong. But I no longer wanted to discuss it with Graham. Not today. The truth was that Tristan and I did have a connection, one I'd never experienced with anyone besides Graham before, but nothing had happened with him, and nothing would happen.

"Harper, don't be mad."

I wasn't mad. I was sad. Why couldn't he understand that? The man I loved had been unfaithful, however "accidental" it had been, and that wasn't easy to get over. "I'll see about coming to you," I said. "I need to see you."

"That'd be great."

Silence dragged out between us as I searched my brain for something to say.

Again, there was a commotion on his end, and his eyes left the screen. "Stop it, you guys," he said.

That brought them around to the front of Graham's laptop where I could see them. Two of his roommates and a couple female soldiers. They all waved at me. I didn't know any of them well, not like I'd known his friends back in the States. They were joking and shoving each other and Graham. Obviously, they were close. A pit opened in my stomach.

One of the women said something I couldn't hear, and they all laughed. "Look, I gotta go," Graham said. "I'll call you tomorrow, okay?"

He was usually off on Sundays, working only one each month. "Okay sounds good."

"I love you," he added.

I kissed my finger and placed it on the screen as he disappeared, the call disconnecting. "I love you too," I whispered.

I did love him, but how long had it been since my knees felt weak when he looked at me? How long since I'd cried into my pillow because the ache of missing him was so strong? I swallowed hard, trying to remember. Certainly not since he'd told me about the woman. Love was more difficult when we were looking at one another through screens, but I had felt that way once, hadn't I? I knew I hadn't imagined it, yet now it was as if a wall encased my heart where Graham was concerned.

That's it, I thought. *I'm just protecting myself.* Everything would change once we were together again. I had to trust myself. Leaving my phone on a couch in my sitting room, I hurried downstairs.

Everyone was already in the dining room, waiting for me. As I appeared, Rosina signaled the cook, who lurked in the far doorway where the dining room intersected the kitchen. Tristan smiled at me and winked, sending warmth flooding through my body, so unlike the numbness I'd felt with Graham.

I told myself it was because Tristan was convenient and attentive. As promised, he'd been a gentleman, but now with his girlfriend here, maybe the tension that occasionally cropped up between us like some ungrounded electric wire could be put to rest once and for all.

Dinner began as a polite disaster. Besides the longing looks she cast toward Tristan and the penetrating ones directed at me, Jianne was quiet and docile. Tristan, seeming to feel the burden of Jianne's stare, concentrated on his food. That left me and Rosina to carry the conversation.

Fortunately, she was a practiced hostess and soon had me forgetting my awkwardness as she questioned me about my family, my work, and how I'd met Mel. She didn't ask me about my fiancé or future plans, and Tristan didn't mention it either, so I kept silent. It felt a little dishonest, especially with how obvious it was that Tristan and Jianne had history between them, but not enough for me to steer the conversation in that direction.

Rosina also shared stories of Tristan growing up: pranks he'd played on his sisters, his sudden "allergy" to piano when he'd grown tired of lessons, and how he'd failed his first English class. With her tales, I could imagine Tristan growing up here.

By the time they served the main course, Tristan had joined the conversation, and during dessert—a lovely chocolate mousse pie—even Jianne contributed a few sentences.

After dinner, Rosina glanced at the phone in the little purse she carried and said to Tristan, "I'd better get going. Your father will be expecting me, and we still need to drive Jianne home. I'll be back early in the week." She shifted her gaze to include me. "I can't wait to see the final plans."

"We'll walk you out." Tristan led the way with his mother, and somehow I found Jianne by my side. I wondered if her lagging behind was on purpose, if she'd warn me to stay away from Tristan, even though Mel said she'd been the one who gave him up.

Sure enough, Jianne stopped in the main hall and looked at me expectantly. "Um," she began. "I—um . . . well . . ."

Tension built inside me. What could be so life-shattering that she needed all those false starts? I opened my mouth to explain everything, but she beat me to it after all.

"If you would allow me, I would like to help with the redesign," she said.

I stared at her, blinking my eyes twice. Had I heard correctly?

"Taking away some of the furniture . . . I always thought that would be a good idea." She glanced at the others who had reached the front doors, where no butler was in sight. I hoped he was somewhere with his family. "I would like to learn from you, if that is all right."

This was her request? I'd expected a demand—no, rather a shy plea, given her apparent nature—for me to stay away from Tristan. This was a complete surprise.

Unless this was the only way she felt she could keep an eye on us.

"Okay," I said. "I can always use an extra body—if you aren't afraid to get a little dirty." I eyed her red dress, wondering if she planned to show up every night garbed like that, pretending to work so she could pursue Tristan. "You should wear jeans, or shorts, or something casual."

Her next words surprised me more. "I'll come during the day." She looked down and added so softly I almost didn't hear, "When it's just us."

Did she mean when Tristan was at work? "You can come

anytime, but I won't be working too late anyway, and I'm sure the workmen I hire will keep their regular hours."

"Thank you." She looked up and gave me a tremulous smile before hurrying to join Rosina at the door.

"See you tomorrow at dinner?" Rosina was saying to Tristan.

"Of course." Tristan gave his mother and Jianne kisses on their cheeks, and afterward I had to do the same. I usually enjoyed this Beaumontian custom, but tonight it felt weird, especially without knowing how Jianne fit into Tristan's life. Not that it was any of my business.

Tristan stood on the porch watching as Rosina's driver opened the door to her car and the two women slid gracefully inside. Seconds later they were only a set of taillights heading down the road. He let out a lengthy sigh, as if he'd been holding it in a long time.

I wanted to ask him about Jianne, but it wasn't really my place, especially if I didn't want to answer questions about Graham.

"It's a beautiful evening," he said, staring into the sky where bands of colored clouds painted the horizon.

"Yes, it is." I couldn't imagine anything more perfect. The evening was warm and without a breeze, yet not too stifling, caught in that magical time just after sunset and before the real darkness set in.

He turned to me, his head tilted, his smile wide. "We could take a dip. I think there were several swimming cost—uh, suits— in that closet."

"Sorry, I don't swim."

His eyes opened wide. "You don't swim? No way. Who doesn't swim?"

"Me. I don't know how." My hands curled into fists at my side. I should have known I wouldn't be able to keep that from him, not if I stayed here. "I don't even own a swimsuit."

"Really? I mean, what did you do on all those hot California nights?"

"Stayed inside under the air conditioning." I'd had enough questions for one day. "You know what? I'm really tired. I think I'll turn in."

I walked inside, trying not to hurry too fast so he wouldn't wonder if my retreat had more to do with the pool than my exhaustion. After the turmoil of today and last night, the only thing I wanted was to crash into that bed upstairs and sleep for twelve hours.

He hurried to catch up to me. "Forget swimming, how about a movie in my awesome theater?"

My steps slowed as I looked over at him. His voice had been casual, but he stood with his hands clenched a bit awkwardly in front of him, as if my response mattered. Probably my imagination. But a movie did sound nice, and it would keep me from obsessing over my relationship with Graham.

"That depends," I said. "Do you have popcorn?"

Tristan

*S*omething was up with Harper and swimming. I'd seen it in her eyes when we'd been out on the deck, but I'd thought she simply wanted to jump in the water to cool off. Now I could see the reluctance, not only in her face but in every line of her body. How anyone could reach adulthood without learning to swim was something I couldn't begin to imagine, but then I'd been born into a society of lesson-crazed mothers. At any rate, her reaction wasn't normal. She was both fascinated and repelled.

Maybe I could teach her to swim. The idea was extremely compelling—if I could get her to agree. Spending time with Harper, especially in a swimming costume, would be more than pleasant.

"*Princess Bride* then?" I asked as we entered the theater room, which boasted five rows of comfortable bucket seats, a bar with a microwave and fridge along the back, and a curved movie screen that filled the entire wall.

"Yes. Great." She wandered down the rows of seats. "This is both impressive and very . . ." She flushed slightly and didn't finish. She didn't have to. It *was* very intimate, as if we were the only people in the entire world. But somehow I felt that way a lot when I was with her.

I pushed in the movie, grabbed our snacks, dimmed the lights, and followed her down to the second row. It was nice not to decide where to sit for a change. Most of the women I'd dated waited for me to choose.

She accepted the drink and unscrewed the lid. "Just so you know, Jianne asked to help with the redesign."

I dropped the popcorn in her lap, spilling a handful of kernels. "Oh, sorry. But did you say she *asked* to help?"

"Does that bother you?" Harper started sweeping up the popcorn with her hands.

"No. But it surprises me." It was good sign actually. A really good sign.

"I didn't know if it would upset you, since she broke up with you." Before I could respond, Harper groaned and rushed on. "Sorry. It was her that you were dating last, wasn't it? Yes, I'm guilty of listening to the rumor mill."

Even in the dim light she looked so flustered it made me laugh. I wanted to tell her the truth, but letting everyone think it was Jianne who'd broken up with me was another way to protect her. A few choice statements in the right ears and assumptions by even those closest to me had assured she wouldn't suffer any stigma from the breakup.

"There was a lot involved," I said. "Jianne is a sweet girl—woman. I'm not holding a candle for her, if that's what you're asking." I don't know why I had to make sure she knew that. "We were never engaged or anything. We dated about six months."

Harper's eyes narrowed, as if contemplating my truthfulness.

Thankfully, the opening credits were over, and I could focus on the movie screen. It was the perfect date movie, silly enough to make fun of but smart enough to be interesting. When it was over, neither of us made a move to leave.

"We could watch another," I said. "Maybe a guy flick. You know, something like *The Terminator*."

She laughed. "Seriously?"

"Okay, something else then."

She covered a yawn. "Actually, I'd love to, but I think I'd better not. I can barely keep my eyes open."

If we'd been dating I would have cuddled her in my arms and urged her to fall asleep while we watched another movie.

Stop it.

"Okay, but I need to give you something first."

She followed me along the hallway to the master suite. "Wow, and I thought my room was elegant. You know the furniture is all too crowded in here too. Beautiful though, and I love the blue shades here."

"That's why I thought they would look nice in the ballroom."

"No way." She gave me a smile that softened the response. "You'll love what I have planned. Trust me."

I did, and in a way I never would have if she had caved to my ideas.

I walked into the other room and retrieved a blue T-shirt from the closet. "I know how you feel about borrowing my sister's things, so this should work for tonight."

"Thank you."

I walked with her back to her room, and there we paused. The tension built again so thickly that it was hard to swallow. I wanted to kiss her, to demand that she reconsider her engagement. To ask if she had any feelings for me at all. Because regardless of what I'd been telling myself—that she was here only to redecorate or to stop my mother's matchmaking—when it came right down to it, none of that was true. Maybe it never had been.

"Goodnight," she said softly.

"Goodnight."

It was all I could do to continue smiling as she went in and shut the door firmly behind her.

Chapter 11

Harper

Emerson showed up the next morning in biker leather, talking and laughing as always, but there was also a sadness in his eyes. Tristan and I were in the sunny breakfast nook with an array of pastries. That man certainly knew what I liked.

"What's wrong?" I asked Emerson when Tristan excused himself to see that my luggage was taken upstairs.

"Stefania left for England."

"It's not like you won't see her again. I Skype with Graham all the time."

"I know." He blew out a breath. "But she doesn't need me, not like I want her to. And believe me, I pulled out all the stops. Romantically speaking, that is."

That meant a lot. Hanging with me and Mel, Emerson knew about romance and what women liked. We'd made sure to educate him. Someday his future wife would thank us.

"I was hoping she'd want to transfer to the States," he added.

"She's still young. You can't expect her to give up everything she's planned her entire life. Give her some time."

"That's just it. I think time will only come between us."

I set my fork down. "What aren't you telling me?"

"I'm pretty sure she's attracted to someone else."

"Oh, no. That guy she was dancing with?"

"No, that guy's cousin. Or something." He sighed. "It's really okay. I had no intention of getting involved with anyone until I was established in my career anyway. I think it's just with you and Mel both getting married, I sort of fell into wanting a relationship." A teasing note had entered his voice. "All that sickening romance seems to be catching."

"Oh, you poor baby." Now this was more what I expected from Emerson. Ever since his acne had disappeared in college, he'd been dating more women than I could keep track of. Those killer green eyes, surfer boy good looks, and a brain that helped him graduate at the top of his engineering class at Stanford were an irresistible combination.

Unless you were Stefania apparently.

"You didn't bring my luggage on your bike, did you?"

"No, it wouldn't fit. Mel made me bring two whole suitcases." He reached for a pastry. "But I'm having someone drive my bike up here for me."

"Why?"

"Because you can't stay here alone with this guy, however nice he is. Mel tells me his mother doesn't live here anymore and that he was just dumped. In good conscience, I can't leave you here alone."

"Oh, brother."

He grinned. "Okay, Lucida asked me to stay and keep an eye on you." He rolled his eyes. "I just can't tell her no. Besides, you can probably use an extra hand."

"What about your job?"

"I have three weeks to be back home or they give it to someone else. Truthfully, I've been thinking about staying here and working on the royal building projects with Mel. Or finding something here on my own. With Kami and Mel's connections, there are numerous options, and being in Beaumont is a one-time opportunity. Most guys my age don't get to experience Europe like this."

I saluted him with my fork. "Broken heart and all."

"Broken heart and all."

"Who has a broken heart?" Tristan said, sauntering into the room.

"Me," Emerson said with a laugh. "But it'll pass. It always does."

"I hope so." Tristan's expression looked distant, and I wondered if he was thinking of Jianne. I didn't exactly buy the no-torch thing, because I felt he was hiding something about her. Maybe over the next few weeks I could see if there was anything I could do to help them reconnect. At least he seemed okay with her coming to help me.

Tristan remained standing by the table, his hands clasped together in front of him as he had when he'd asked me to watch the movie and later when he'd walked me to my room. I was beginning to suspect it signaled nervousness. "So my mother invited us all to Sunday dinner, which is actually a late lunch. It's a family tradition."

I wanted to say no because I was anxious to get started on my designs, but the way his hands clenched and the warmth of his voice changed my mind. "We'd love to. Right, Emerson?"

"Sure. As long as no one makes me eat pigs' ears."

I scowled at him.

"Hey, I'm just saying."

Tristan was laughing again, dropping into a chair, his hands relaxed. "No pigs' ears. I promise."

"You'll need to change," I told Emerson. "You'll roast in that leather." I looked down at my skort, now paired with Tristan's shirt which almost covered it completely. "I'll need to change too."

We passed the afternoon with Tristan's parents and his teenage brother, and then with a sightseeing jaunt around the town, including the cathedral where Tristan's family still attended church.

Then I made the mistake of telling Emerson about Tristan's castle, and he insisted that we show him. That ate up the rest of the afternoon and evening, but it was a perfect, wonderful day. Emerson's presence had completely nullified the tension between us. No more impromptu dances or almost kisses. No more worrying if my feelings were betraying Graham.

By the time we returned to the house, I'd done absolutely nothing on the project, but it had been the best day I could remember in a long time.

Emerson's bike arrived, and he went for a night ride after dinner while Tristan and I sipped more sweet tea on the deck by the pool. The night was muggy, without a single breeze, and the water beckoned. I shivered and looked away.

"I got something for you." Tristan jumped to his feet and disappeared inside the house. He came back shortly carrying a large paper shopping bag. Sitting on the chair next to me, he withdrew something orange wrapped in clear plastic cellophane.

"You bought this today? How? I saw your whole town. Practically everything was shut down except that little mall." We'd also been together the entire day, except for a short time before breakfast and after when I'd changed.

"I have a friend who owns a boutique. She dropped these off for me."

These? That sounded plural.

"Go ahead," he urged.

I ripped the plastic, and a silky swimming suit fell out into my hands.

"I remembered what you said about gold being your color, and I thought since you'll be here for a while, I could teach you how to swim."

His tone was matter-of-fact, and not at all pushy, but my throat clogged with fear. I wanted to throw the suit in his face and run inside, but his elbows rested on his knees as he leaned toward me, his hands clenched together. Definitely nervous.

"Is something wrong?" he asked. "Do you hate it?" He reached in the bag for another package, ripping it open and tossing it to me. Then another. In all there were a dozen suits: one-pieces, bikinis, tankinis, and everything in between. "You can pick which ones you like."

He waited for several more heartbeats. "Look, if you don't want to, forget it. I just thought that you might want . . . swimming comes in handy when you go on a boating trip or when you take kids to the waterpark . . ."

He was right. My fear of water had made me miss out on numerous experiences. I had never swum in the ocean with Mel or gone waterskiing with Graham. I'd never be able to teach any children I might have how to swim.

"You're right," I said. "I need to learn. It's a good idea." The more I considered it, the more I wanted to shed my fear. No one was here to mock my efforts—well, except Emerson, and we'd been friends too long for him to count. Tristan might tease, but soon I would never see him again.

"I'll try them on." I tossed the suits into the shopping bag.

"We'll start tomorrow after work. I'll probably be late, but there should be time after dinner."

I was just happy he hadn't said today. I needed to work myself up to it mentally.

Tristan shot me another anxious look. "If you don't want to—"

I wished he'd stop treating me like I might break, because I was strong, and it was high time I conquered my past. "I do. With or without you, I'm going into that pool tomorrow."

"I saw pictures of you from the engagement party," Graham said a short time later from the screen of my laptop. "You were dancing with that guy you mentioned. You didn't tell me he was a prince."

I snuggled back into the soft leather couch in my sitting room. "I didn't think it mattered. I mean, his grandfather was once king, so that makes him a prince, at least here in Beaumont. He's also a duke."

"So is he in line for the crown?" Graham's voice was tight and his face was rigid. What was wrong with him?

"Not directly. Tristan's father was only the second son of the king, and the first son has four children, one of which is Gabriel—the current king. Tristan is Gabriel's first cousin, but unless a plague comes along and wipes out all of Gabriel's family, including his twin brother, Tristan's not in line for anything. And even then it would go to his father first."

"There were dozens of pictures," Graham said. "You're all over the online gossip columns. The only other woman he's shown with is Stefania."

I couldn't decide if his tone was hurt or accusatory. "Well, I can't help what pictures they post, but it was just dancing in a roomful of people. It wasn't anything. He's a very nice man, though. I like him."

"This isn't to get me back for last month, is it?" Graham asked. "I told you I'm sorry. I know I can't take back what happened, but I won't do it again."

Pain reverberated through my chest. "This has nothing to do with you cheating on me. I wanted to dance, that's all. It could have been you I was with, but you chose not to come."

His jaw clenched. "What if we weren't engaged? Would you be interested in him?"

I was honest enough to admit to myself that I would be interested in Tristan if I weren't engaged, but telling Graham that would be destructive. "What does that matter? I chose to stay with you even after what you did. I know how much something like that hurts, and I'd break it off with us if I decided there was someone else. You need to trust me."

He finally sat back, his face relaxing. "Okay, I do trust you."

At least we had that much. I'd never given him reason to doubt my fidelity in the two years we'd dated. "It's him I don't trust," Graham added, destroying the moment.

"Well, he's been nothing but a gentleman."

For a second, the memory of Tristan coming closer to me in the castle flashed in my memory. I was even more glad now that nothing had happened, not even a mistake I'd have to confess to Graham.

Graham moved closer to the screen. "In the pictures . . . you looked happy." His voice was strained on the last words.

"You know how I love dancing."

"I know." He sighed, sitting back in his chair. "I blame this on myself. I should have kept my promise to visit."

"Yes, you should have. But I'm not angry." Not anymore.

He sighed. "Harper, is everything okay between us? I mean, besides the fact that I've kind of been a total jerk."

I didn't know the answer to that, or at least I wasn't sure. How could I tell with all the space between us? He lived his life, and I lived mine, crossing only during our electronic chats. Once, we'd fit into each other's worlds perfectly, and I couldn't imagine life without him, but after the long months apart, maybe we'd both changed.

"I'm not sure. Maybe we just need to spend more time together. It'll be better after the wedding." My throat felt suddenly dry.

"I scheduled my leave next month, but you could come here before so we can spend time together after my shifts."

Relief settled over me. This was something I could focus on. "Okay. I'll do a rush on this project, and even if I'm not finished in a couple weeks, I can get to a point where I can take a break." At least I hoped Tristan wouldn't mind. "Maybe I could stay in Germany until you have leave, and then we can spend your leave together here. I'd like to show you around."

"Actually, I'd hoped we could go back to the States. I'll have two and a half more days accrued by then, plus an extra bonus day they gave me for attending that optional exercise. That gives me enough time to go home, and my parents will pay for the ticket."

That's right. His parents and friends were all back in the States. He would only know Mel and Emerson here in Beaumont. He had no idea how witty Kami was, or that Gabriel loved setting aside his kingly duties to beat his cousins in arm wrestles. He hadn't seen how kindly Damien treated me, and maybe I'd forgotten to tell him that Lucida had become my second mother. He couldn't imagine how beautiful the countryside was, or how intriguing the architecture, especially ancient castles that hadn't been lived in for a century. Pastries, olive oil, and pasta to die for—I wanted to share it all with him. Until this moment, I never dreamed he wouldn't be interested.

Graham was staring at me anxiously. "I mean, if you want we can go there. But don't you want to see your parents?"

I'd seen my parents only a week ago, and they were coming back for Mel's wedding. They'd been talking about buying a vacation rental here. Maybe I should tell this to Graham, but after our discussion, it somehow felt . . . futile.

"We can talk details later," I said.

His eyes left the screen. "Hey, the guys are here. Gotta go."

"Goodbye. I love you."

This time it was him who kissed the screen, while I reached out and pushed the disconnect button. I stared at the computer feeling empty and alone.

Harper

By the time I showered and dressed the next morning, Tristan had already left. I'd worn his shirt to bed again because I'd been too lazy to unpack more than the outfit I'd worn to his parents' house. The shirt also happened to be made from what must be the softest material in the world. I liked how I felt it in.

To my surprise, Emerson was already waiting on the main floor. I handed him a measuring tape and directed him to put the dimensions into the program that would generate an accurate rendition. That would save me hours. Both he and Mel had graduated in structural engineering and not interior design, but they were familiar with the program I used. As a computer enthusiast, Emerson probably knew it better than I did.

While he worked, I began categorizing the furniture, using post-it notes to determine what would stay, what would be transferred to another room, and what would go into storage. Jianne, dressed in faded jeans and a fitted blouse, appeared before I'd finished one room. I immediately put her to work helping me, but we hadn't been at it more than thirty minutes when I realized Jianne had a solid understanding of furniture and design.

"So, where did you learn about design?" I asked.

She smiled and met my gaze. "I graduated in history, but I had a lot of design classes at the University as well. That's how Tristan and I started dating, actually. We went on a tour of one of his factories and we discovered our parents knew each other. His mother found out I'd been there and invited us to a charity event. We started dating after that."

Their dating after the event might explain the shadow on Tristan's face when he'd trailed off after telling me he'd had fun at Mel's party. Maybe he'd remembered meeting Jianne a similar event, one where he'd fallen in love with her. I shook my head to clear the thoughts.

"Sorry about you two breaking up." I could have bitten my tongue even as I said it. She looked down, the excitement draining from her.

"It was my fault."

Her fault?

"Well, maybe it's not too late."

She didn't reply, and she was saved from further discussion when Emerson came into the room to ask a question. I stopped and introduced them. As usual, Emerson perked up around Jianne the way he did around any attractive new woman, but Jianne didn't react to him. I finally shooed him away so we could get back to work.

After we finished categorizing all the furniture on the main floor, we did a quick run through the bedrooms, marking a few pieces that really needed to be grouped with similar furniture downstairs. Then we braved the storage room, where we both became covered in dust.

When we unearthed the set of ancient furniture I'd seen with Tristan, Jianne rubbed her fingers along the wood trim. "Oh, these should be in one of those old castles, you know? Like those pieces you want removed from the drawing room."

"Exactly what I was thinking. But for now I'm considering using them in one of the smaller drawing rooms as sort of an era display. Or maybe in the library."

"That would be wonderful." She smiled and didn't quite meet my eyes as she added, "Thank you for letting me help. I've really enjoyed myself today."

She was too sweet. How could Tristan not see how much they had in common? At least about furniture. Maybe getting them back together was my real mission here.

Whatever my plan, Jianne was long gone before Tristan made it home, even though he arrived well before dinner. "You're early," I said.

He grinned as if he knew a secret. "I brought you something." From behind his back he took out an inflatable swim ring.

"You've got to be kidding."

Wading into the pool wasn't the problem, but anything after waist deep was huge. My already pounding heartbeat changed to an uneven rhythm that had me seeing stars. The voices and memories that came into my head were worse.

Screaming, shouting, pleading with God. My mother's reddened eyes and my father's somber face as he explained about my brother and how he wouldn't be coming home from where the ambulance had taken him. The tiny coffin and the unmoving face of a boy that no longer looked like the brother I loved.

An arm came around me, and I felt the warmth of Tristan's body against mine. "Easy," he murmured. "Just hold onto me for a moment. Let yourself float. You can't drown here. Besides, I'm an excellent swimmer, and I know mouth to mouth."

I couldn't help looking at his mouth then. The voices faded, and my heart resumed its regular pounding—if an entire orchestra in my chest could be called regular. Tristan's bare chest was a wonderful mixture of strength and heat.

"See?" he said. "Really, the trick with swimming is all about getting in the water. Because even moving your hands a bit like this"—he showed me a swirling motion with one hand, while the other still held me close—"will keep a person up. Now stretch out your legs a bit and kick your feet while I hold onto you. You don't have to grip me so tight. I promise, I won't let you go."

I was all too aware of his arm around my middle, and I was grateful I'd chosen the first suit he'd given me so my stomach was covered. However, my heart didn't seem to think that thin material was enough of a barrier.

After five minutes, Tristan asked me to rotate to my back. "Learning to float will give you a lot more confidence." So he had me tilting the top of my head into the water, pushing my feet down, and puffing my chest up. I was more than a little self-conscious, but when I succeeded staying up on the first try, I hugged him, glad the water on my face masked any tears.

"I should have done this before," I said.

He shrugged. "You're doing it now."

"Wait until Mel sees me."

For another half hour I stayed in the water, grasping the inflated ring with one arm and paddling with the other, kicking my legs to push myself across the length of the pool. Tristan swam easily beside me, a ready anchor I could depend on.

He wrapped a huge white towel around me as we climbed out and settled on two lawn chairs. The sky was darkening enough that stars were starting to come out. It was so peaceful and beautiful, and I was struck with the strong realization that I was going to miss Beaumont when I left.

My eyes drifted to Tristan, and I had a sneaking suspicion that the beautiful evenings and the mouth-watering pastries weren't the only things I was going to miss.

Tristan

I didn't want the moment to end. I could happily sit on the deck forever and talk to Harper. I understood that she was off-limits, but I told myself that as long as I remained a gentleman, she would never suspect how I was falling for her. And falling I was. Like a man plunging off a cliff carrying a bag of rocks into the depths of the sea, a fate I couldn't possibly hope to survive.

"How'd it go in the house today?" I asked.

"Oh, that's right." She sat up, the towel falling off to reveal the curve of her shoulder. "I have one of the renditions ready. Emerson helped, so I was able to finish the ballroom design."

I couldn't help chuckling. "Why am I not surprised you did that one first?"

"Well, we did get the furniture figured out as well, and all the dimensions are in the computer for the other rooms. I have to finalize designs and order the materials, but if you sign off on the ballroom, I'm ready for a crew to start work. Did your secretary have any luck finding someone?"

"Yes. They were booked for weeks, but when they learned it was at our family residence, they managed to squeeze us in."

She found that amusing. "Of course they did."

"They can be here by Thursday. My secretary has probably emailed you their information by now, including their hourly rates. I also have a person at my factory for the reupholstering, and he can be here as soon as tomorrow, if you like."

"Oh, I like," she said. "So far there are sixteen pieces I want re-covered. As soon as you approve the material, I'll put him to work."

The way she said "Oh, I like" sent an ache through my gut. I could imagine her staring up at me—wanting me like that. I jumped to my feet, knowing that action was the best method to push the image from my mind. "Well, show me then."

Laughing, she pulled on a pair of shorts, and we went upstairs to her sitting room. We sat together on a couch, and with a few taps on her laptop screen, she brought up the 3D images she had created of the ballroom. She hadn't put in the extensive trim, but it was obviously the same room. Instead of the heavy red, there was now light-colored wallpaper with threads of red and gold. Dramatic lighting and wall tapestries made it a completely different room—a room that felt made for dancing.

"Lightening it up gives it a more modern feel while keeping true to the era of the original," she said, as if trying to convince me.

"I agree. I'm glad you didn't go with my suggestion of blue."

"The blue would only have worked if we changed all the gold to silver, but that would have completely ruined the original feel. Gold has always been important in history. Its popularity comes and goes, depending on whether gold prices are high or low, but

I don't think anyone should ruin a perfectly good room because silver happens to be all the rage at the moment. Give it another few years and the tide will turn again. Meanwhile, you'll have this beautiful room that still matches the architecture." Her eyes flashed with her words, and her entire face was vibrant and alive. I couldn't look away.

"This is also where I want nine of the reupholstered pieces," she continued, one finger running across the laptop. "To intersperse with the existing pieces. I plan to use an off-white material that hints of gold and has subtle red designs through it. Elegant without being too obvious. The company that makes the material is in Italy, but they promise overnight delivery."

She brought up an image of the material. If her description didn't have me convinced, the picture did. "It's perfect," I said. "Let's go with it."

"I haven't told you how much it'll cost. I emailed you a bid, but I didn't know the going rate for the workmen, so it's not exact."

I brought up her email on my phone, scanning it quickly. "I'm good with this. Even the outer range seems conservative, though. We should up that by ten percent, and let me know if you need more. But what's this notation about taking out a wall?"

She clicked a few menus, and the image on her screen changed to the computer rendition of my office—or it somewhat looked like my office.

"It's missing a wall," I pointed out.

"I'm not finished with the mockup, but how would you feel about opening the room more and incorporating that little sitting room next door? It's not really being used for anything. Then you could have a nice set of couches in your office to meet with business acquaintances and even serve refreshments. We could add larger windows as well. I got the idea from Damien's office. He works a lot from home these days now that he's marrying Mel."

"That would come in handy—especially once the house is full of kids again."

She sat back, all at once looking rather tired, as if showing me her plans had exhausted her. "I bet it was nice having your siblings around while you were growing up."

"Well, I'm a lot older than my siblings. My parents had me too young, and they were trying to figure out me and married life, so they waited eight years to have my sisters. But the house was always full of cousins, or I was at one of their houses. My father didn't get much work accomplished here because we always interrupted him."

"Sounds wonderful growing up with all those cousins."

I met Harper's gaze, noting the sadness in her eyes. Too late, I remembered she was an only child. "Do you have cousins?"

"Two. But we're not close. Where I'm from people don't really have a lot of kids. I had friends growing up, of course, but Mel is my best friend, and we didn't meet until college. And Emerson is like—" She broke off, her hands clenching in her lap.

"The brother you never had?"

The next moment her eyes were full of tears that soon spilled over as she wiped at them furiously.

"What's wrong?"

"Nothing. Sorry." She wiped some more. "I haven't gotten much sleep, and it's been a long day, and—"

I scooted closer to her on the couch, taking her laptop from her and placing it on the coffee table. "Tell me. Please. I'd like to help."

She stopped wiping away the tears and let them slide down her face. "It was a long time ago, but the swimming . . . I had a brother—Josh. Younger than me. He drowned when he was three. No one knows how he got out of the house or unlocked the gate. There was a chair beside it—he was so smart."

The air whooshed out of my chest at the revelation. No wonder she was afraid of the water. No wonder she didn't swim. "I'm sorry I forced you—"

"You didn't force me. You asked, and I agreed to learn. I *needed* to learn."

That's right, she wasn't Jianne, and breaking down as she told me about her brother didn't mean I'd pushed too hard. I hoped.

"Anyway," she continued, "he would have graduated from high school last year. I think that's why my mother started traveling so much. You know, all those graduation announcements from her friends who had babies at the same time."

"I bet that was tough on you. You were how old?"

"Six. For a long time I didn't really understand. Even at the funeral, I kept thinking he didn't look like my brother, so maybe it wasn't him and he'd come back. My mother refused to let me go swimming, of course, and after a few months we moved to a house without a pool."

"How'd that make you feel?" I ached to dry her tears, to hold her, but I didn't want to take advantage of her, and I wasn't quite sure if I did touch her that I would be able to let her go. I needed to be strong for both of us.

"At first I was relieved, then after missing so many pool parties, I got angry, but that sort of settled into fear of the water—as you saw tonight." She gave a wry smile that seemed to stop the tears. "As a teen it was hard."

"I guess in California, it's all about the beach and swim parties."

That elicited a sad ghost of a smile. "Right. I didn't dare go to the beach with friends because guys loved to throw girls in the water. But my mom made up for it. If someone held a pool or beach party, she held a party at an ice rink or an amusement park. She bought horses and had all the kids over. Spent more money than she should have. After a while it didn't matter. I didn't tell people about it, and I don't think anyone ever guessed. Mel's the only one I ever told."

"Not Emerson?"

"He knows I don't swim, but not why. And he really is a brother to me. His kids and Mel's will be my kids' cousins."

I became aware of our bare legs touching, of how we were both still dressed for swimming. She was staring at me wide-eyed. Did she feel it? The attraction between us?

"That's why it's going to be hard to have Mel stay here after I leave." She wiped her hands over her face, whisking away the remaining tears. "Good thing she has money to visit me. I don't know that Graham and I will be so fortunate. My parents are well off, but we're both barely starting out in our careers."

Her words effectively placed a barrier between us, every bit as strong as if she'd moved away physically.

"I hope the proceeds from this job will ease that transition and help you begin your marriage." I arose and started across the carpet to hide the bitterness I felt.

The jealousy.

"Tristan." Harper jumped up.

I turned to her perhaps a bit too eagerly. "What?"

"Thank you. For getting me in the water. It means a lot."

Just like that all my bitterness seeped away. "You're welcome. I guess I'll go shower and change. See you tomorrow?"

"Or we could watch another movie. If you're up to it."

Her dark hair was still wet and shiny, her face splotched with red, her eyes slightly swollen, but she was beautiful to me, and I couldn't resist the plea in her eyes. She didn't want to be alone right then. Maybe it was because of her brother, or maybe it was something else.

I didn't want to be alone either.

"As you wish," I said, in reference to our last movie choice. "I'll meet you in the theater in fifteen minutes. First one there gets to choose the film."

She groaned. "No fair; my hair takes longer to wash. I guess we're watching *The Terminator.*"

Harper

The next few days fell into a routine: working all day with Emerson and Jianne, dinner with Tristan—mostly just the two of us because Emerson usually went out with friends—and then private swim lessons in the pool. These were almost always followed by a movie with Tristan and sometimes Emerson if he came home from his partying soon enough.

By the time the first Thursday arrived, I had the designs ready, the wallpaper and other materials delivered, and we'd stripped half of the old paper from the ballroom ourselves. Contrary to his initial comments, Tristan never seemed to work late, and he had come home early several times to find me covered in dust or paint, with bits of old wallpaper in my hair.

Once the workmen arrived, the project began in earnest. Six men showed up, and I started five of them on the ballroom while I went over the designs with their supervisor, who thankfully spoke decent English, unlike his men. He expressed approval of my designs, and I breathed a sigh of relief when the only suggestion he had was to tear out the false ceiling in the drawing room.

"I didn't even know it had a false ceiling," I admitted.

His weathered face crinkled deeply around his eyes when he smiled. "It was all the rage some decades ago, before Prince Fontaine's parents married. But the originals are much better. I bet it has detailed crown molding underneath."

"If it doesn't, we'll add some." I took a hammer to the ceiling myself. Sure enough, the real ceiling was a good foot above the fake one.

After the first week, I spent most of my time deciding where to use the workmen next and checking on Tristan's upholstery guy, who was super slow but the best I'd ever seen. I put Jianne and Emerson in charge of directing furniture placement according to my designs. Emerson was hopeless at it, but Jianne had a talent for keeping him in line.

Over the days, I'd watched Jianne open up, and I felt she'd become a friend. Sometimes I tried to steer the conversation to Tristan, to see if her feelings for him had changed, but it was difficult with Emerson there. Twice, she'd accepted my invitation to dinner at Tristan's, but the two of them never exchanged anything more than the most casual words. Most of the time, she wouldn't even meet his gaze, which puzzled me because I eagerly looked forward to each evening when Tristan walked through the door. I loved splashing him in the pool and arguing over which movie to watch.

Two weeks after beginning the project, the ballroom was completed except regrouting and resealing of the stone floor. The drawing room was also nearly finished. Emerson and I gave each other a high five while Jianne laughed at us.

"Let's call it a day," Emerson said. "Come on, Jianne. I'll take you home." He'd been giving her a ride to her aunt's house while her car was in the shop, and I was glad they'd become friends. Jianne had lost much of her shyness, at least with us.

"All right," Jianne said. "But I know you really just want to see if my aunt saved any of the spaghetti from last night."

He grinned. "Busted!"

I watched them go before deciding to take a break myself. There was something I wanted to do. Slipping upstairs, I changed into one of the two swimsuits I'd kept from those Tristan had delivered. I called Mel when I was ready.

"What are you doing?" I asked.

"Talking to you."

"No, seriously." I tucked my laptop under my arms and started down the staircase. "Do you have a minute?"

"Sure, I'm at the palace with Kami right now. Lucida went out of town, and you know how she is about me staying at Damien's without her there."

"That woman is all about chaperones. Emerson told me she asked him to stay here and keep an eye on me."

Mel laughed. "I'm sure she did. I tried to tell her you weren't interested in Tristan that way." She paused. "Uh, Harper? I expected you to jump in right then and tell me I'm right."

I opened my mouth, but nothing emerged.

Another few seconds of silence, and then Mel said, "Oh, no. Really? Did something happen between you two?"

She knew nothing had happened. I talked with her every day—even more than I talked with Graham. "It's just . . . he's not anything like we thought. He has opinions, but he never forces them on me. If anything he's a little too deferential. Sometimes, I wish . . ." Sometimes I wished he would follow through on the stares he gave me. On the desire in his eyes.

There, that was the truth. There was something between us, but I didn't know what he felt about me, so how could I figure out how I felt about him? Or where that put my relationship with Graham. Because deep down I was terrified that Graham would cheat on me again. If not now, then in the future. If he couldn't be faithful for six months apart, what did that say about our chances?

"Harper, are you still there?"

I'd reached the pool area and set the laptop down on the table, keeping the phone jammed against my ear. "Yeah, I am. It's just . . . things with Graham aren't that great. Between you and me, I'm having doubts. I have been for the past month."

"You need to trust your feelings then. Maybe you should go see him. Try to work it out."

"That's actually a great idea." Once I was with Graham, all the doubts would be gone. "I'm at a place in the remodel where I can take a break. The workers would be okay a few days without me."

"Should I ask Damien about using his plane?"

"No. I have to wrap a few things up first. I'll let you know." I held the phone with my shoulder while I opened my laptop. "Now go get on Skype," I said. "There's something I need to show you."

"Is it the ballroom? Did it turn out as well as you thought?"

"It's better than the ballroom. Hurry!"

Minutes later, Mel gave a gasp as she looked out at me from my computer screen and realized what I was wearing. "Is that a swimsuit?"

"Shut up," I said, angling the computer so she could see the pool. Then I jumped in. I wasn't quite ready for diving yet, but I would be soon. I swam across the entire pool and back before jumping out and returning to the computer.

Tears shone in my friend's eyes. "How did you . . . ? When did you . . . ?"

I dabbed at my dripping hair with a towel. "I was keeping it as a surprise. Tristan helped me." I paused and then added, "I told him about Josh. He was really sweet."

"Oh, I wish I was there to hug you right this minute! I'm so happy for you."

"Thank you. I couldn't wait any longer to tell you. You're the only person who really knows what this means to me." Well, maybe her and Tristan.

"What did Graham say when you told him? You know he'll want to take you waterskiing."

I blinked. "Oh, I'm saving it for a surprise."

"You *forgot* to tell him?"

I chewed on my lower lip. "Okay, yeah. But I haven't even told Emerson, and he's been living here. We always wait until he goes out—no, that came out wrong. We don't plan to wait until he leaves, it just works out that way. I swear Emerson has more friends up here now than Tristan does."

"Okay, I understand about Emerson, but why haven't you told Graham?"

I thought about that for a few seconds. Why hadn't I told him? "Well, I think at first it was embarrassing. But it's probably because Graham is already jealous of Tristan. Every time we talk, Graham mentions those pictures he saw of us dancing. What is he going to say when he learns it was Tristan who got me into the water?"

Mel pursed her lips. "Okay, I guess it's my turn to be honest. I think Graham has good reason to be jealous of those pictures. That's why I was so hesitant about you working for Tristan. When you two were dancing together, it was magic, and even the pictures those people posted online show it."

Magic. That was exactly how it had felt—and had every day since. A fairy tale that couldn't possibly be real.

But there was still Graham and our engagement.

"It was just dancing," I said.

Mel's pretty face became stern. "Listen up, Harper, an engagement is for making sure everything is good between a couple—if they're right for each other. An engagement isn't marriage. If you're having any doubts . . . you need to trust yourself. Now what aren't you telling me about Tristan?"

"Well, I really like him." With Tristan there was no past betrayal, no wondering if he'd smash my heart into pieces and expect me to paste it back together.

A movement in my peripheral vision caught my attention, and I glanced up to see Tristan in the doorway that led onto the patio. How much had he heard? "Gotta go," I told Mel.

"Okay. Call me later."

"Bye." I shut the laptop. "You're home early," I said to Tristan.

He came toward me, carrying a white cardboard box I knew was filled with pastries. His smile was warm, and he looked so handsome in his suit that I wanted to stare. "Started without me, huh?" he said. "Have to admit, I feel kind of like a proud father at this moment for teaching you."

I laughed. "I decided to tell Mel. I was going to wait until I was back with her at Damien's or the palace, but I couldn't."

"You miss her, don't you? You can always drive down for a visit, or she can come here."

"I know. We've both been so busy." I reached for the box.

"Uh-uh-uh," he said, shaking his head and holding the box away from me. "They're for our movie tonight."

"You mean they're a bribe. No way am I watching *Terminator 3*. It's my turn to choose."

"Okay, okay. You can choose."

He offered me the pastries, but I set the box on my laptop without opening it. "I'd better wait until after dinner. Carmen said something about salmon and your favorite meal. When are you going to tell her it's codfish you prefer?"

"Never. She's been cooking here since I was a child. Salmon was my favorite back then. I don't want to—how do you say it? Rock the boat. Besides, her salmon is really good." His eyes skimmed down my body. "Uh, you're still dripping. You want another towel?"

Heat rippled through me at his stare. "No, I'm going back into the pool. There's still a little time before dinner."

"I think I've created a monster."

"Oh, yeah?" I grabbed his arm. "Why doesn't this monster throw you into the pool, suit and all?"

"Do you know how much these shoes cost?"

"Take them off then," I taunted.

"No way."

We struggled playfully for a few seconds, his grip slipping on my wet skin. Finally, he scooped me up and tossed me into the pool. I couldn't help noticing that he chose the shallow end and hovered close to the edge for a moment to make sure I was all right.

The next second, Emerson was sprinting toward the pool. "What are you doing!" he shouted. "Harper doesn't know how . . . to . . . hey, when did you learn to swim?"

I finished my lap before pulling myself out of the water. "The past few weeks," I said. "Tristan taught me."

"That's amazing. You should have said you wanted to learn. I'm a good swimmer."

"You're a great swimmer," I corrected. "But what are you doing home so early?"

With a dejected sigh, Emerson dropped into a chair. "I don't know what's wrong with me. Women only see me as a friend."

"That's not true." I grabbed a towel and wrapped it around me. "Women are always calling and hinting about you asking them out."

"Yeah, but the really beautiful ones, the smart ones I'm attracted to, don't think of me romantically. Cases in point: you and Mel."

I rolled my eyes. "Poor baby. Two out of a million. And you aren't even attracted to us." It had taken Emerson and me one date to know we were better as friends.

"It's not only you two." Emerson scowled at me. "Tonight proves that the women I find attractive don't think of me as marriage material. At this rate I'll never get married."

Tristan pulled two patio chairs closer for us to sit next to Emerson. "Tough night, huh?"

"How do you do it?" Emerson asked him.

"Do what?"

"Get them interested? I saw all those women at Mel's party drooling all over you—and their mothers too. Spill the secret, bro."

"Well, money helps," Tristan said a bit dryly, "and the titles."

"No chance of me becoming a prince—what can I do to become a duke? I hear you can buy titles these days."

Tristan laughed. "Not in Beaumont. You inherit them—or sometimes you can marry into them. Anyway, the real secret weapon is your mother."

That caught Emerson's attention. "What?"

"Believe me, it's true. If you have a mother out there broadcasting that she's ready for you to get married so she can have grandbabies, that always gives off marriage material vibes. Then either the women come flocking, or *their* mothers push them to check you out."

"Hmm." Emerson considered that for a moment. "My mother's not here, and I don't think she's all that excited about me becoming serious with anyone. She doesn't want to be a grandmother yet." He looked at me. "Harper, will you do the honors? You know, put out the word."

"No way," I said.

"Why not?"

"Because it would be a total lie. You said yourself that you're not ready to settle down. Women get that vibe. We're not stupid."

His mouth opened with a shock that had to be faked. "I don't know what you're talking about. Marriage might not be my first priority, but of course I'd be ready—as long as it's the *right* woman."

"I don't buy it. Find yourself another mother." I sat back and folded my arms.

"So who's this mystery woman anyway?" Tristan wanted to know.

"Jianne, that's who," Emerson said. "I let her know I was interested, and she practically laughed me out of her aunt's house."

"What?" Tristan and I said together.

"It's true." Emerson wasn't smiling.

"Jianne laughed at you?" Tristan asked. "Jianne Selmone?"

I looked at him sharply to see if he was upset about this new development, but a smile danced around his mouth.

"Yes, that Jianne." Emerson sighed. "What other Jianne do we all know?"

Tristan actually laughed. "Sorry. I'm not mocking you. It's just, you guys have probably noticed that Jianne usually has a hard time expressing herself. It's good she feels she can do that with you. Actually, it's kind of a miracle."

He was right about that because it had taken Jianne a good week to start saying more than a sentence at a time to either me or Emerson. Yet she'd apparently been confident enough to break up with Tristan, so I'd decided she was only shy because she didn't know us. Now Tristan seemed to be implying there was something more to it.

Emerson arose. "Well, that doesn't make me feel any better."

"Where are you going?" I called after him as he started across the deck. "We're about to have dinner."

"Out. Don't wait up. I'm going to a club for a drink or something."

I looked at Tristan. "And just like that, his heart is healed—again."

Tristan's smile made my insides twist. Did he hope that Jianne's rejection of Emerson meant that she secretly still wanted him?

"What?" Tristan said, tilting his head to the side. "What are you thinking when you look at me like that?"

Our eyes held, and suddenly there wasn't enough air in all the world. "I-I'd better dress for dinner."

"Hey, I was thinking about going out tomorrow night," Tristan said. "Maybe we could arrange something with Damien and Mel. That way you two could catch up."

I wanted to go so much that I knew it was a bad idea. We weren't a couple like Mel and Damien, and I was engaged to Graham. "Actually, I've been thinking I'd work only a half day tomorrow and take a quick trip to Germany. Just for the weekend."

"To see Graham." His expression didn't change, but his voice was flat.

Tension grew between us, and I found myself clutching the armrests of my chair.

"Yes. I'd be back Monday or Tuesday at the latest. The workers can survive a day without me."

He nodded slowly. "Of course. That's fine by me."

"Thanks. I didn't think you'd object." But my words mocked me. When I was talking to Mel, it seemed so clear that a trip to see Graham would end the doubts, but now I wasn't sure I wanted to go.

What if I made a mistake that I would regret forever?

Tristan

*S*omehow I made it through dinner, tasting nothing of Carmen's excellent salmon and hearing only half of the conversation with Harper. I'd forgotten all about the finished ballroom and that my mother had asked to see it. She arrived as we were finishing up our meal, and Harper looked relieved, signaling that dinner had been every bit as awkward for her.

I didn't know how to change the awkwardness or how I felt about her visiting her fiancé. The past two weeks having her here, coming home to her each day, had seemed both normal and extraordinary, much like the relationship I'd witnessed with my parents. I could no longer imagine the house without her, or what life had been like before we'd met.

Now she was leaving. Hopefully, that was only temporary, but with her detailed designs and the local crew, her return wasn't necessary or guaranteed. I'd seen women leave their jobs at my factory too many times to count in similar situations. If I were her fiancé, I'd hold her tight and never let her return to Beaumont. Maybe that was why she wanted to leave—because she suspected what I would do if given only a hint that she returned my feelings.

No. Probably her decision had nothing to do with me and everything to do with her feelings for Graham. But how could she love him and look at me the way she sometimes did? As though her real day started each night when I walked through the door.

Unless it was all in my imagination.

One thing I did know is that we couldn't continue the way we were. Graham was always between us, and each day I lost a little more of myself to her and accepted a piece of her in return. I didn't know how much longer I could keep her at arm's length, to be the gentleman I'd promised, and the last thing I wanted to do was hurt her.

These thoughts racing through my head, I followed Harper and my mother into the ballroom. All signs of the renovations were gone, and the place looked as bright and airy as Harper had promised. I could imagine throwing huge parties with all our friends and acquaintances. I could imagine dancing with Harper as the crowd faded from our minds, our eyes fixed only on each other as they had the night we'd met.

"The floor sealing is scheduled for next week," Harper told us, interrupting my daydream. "By then the furniture should be ready."

"I love that raised platform for the orchestra," my mother said. "It really sets off the area. I confess, I was always afraid that someone would dance right into the musicians. And that new lighting along the walls—it changes everything. I can't wait to see the rest of the house."

Harper inclined her head. "I'm glad you approve. You can

peek into the drawing room if you like. We've uncovered a beautiful original ceiling, thanks to the local workers. It's really amazing."

"I'll be sure to look at it on my way out." My mother started across the ballroom toward the door. "First, I want to catch Carmen before she leaves for the day. It's really nice seeing you. I hope you'll come again for dinner this Sunday. And please do bring your friend. He's so charming. It's been wonderful having young people in the house again these past two weeks."

"I'm afraid I won't be able to this Sunday," Harper said. "I'm taking a quick trip to Germany to see my fiancé."

"Oh, that's too bad. We'll miss you." My mother's words came without hesitation, but her eyes slid briefly in my direction, as if to gauge my reaction.

Harper smiled. "Me too. But if you'll excuse me, I should start packing."

"Of course," my mother said.

As soon as Harper disappeared up the stairs, my mother turned in my direction, the frown on her face warning me I was in for some motherly advice. "You're letting her go?"

"Do I have a choice? What else can I do?"

My mother placed her hand on my arm, squeezing as if she could absorb all my sadness. "I've watched you two these past weeks. You've been happier than I've ever seen you. Are you sure this is what you want?"

"I *want* Harper," I said. "But every time I think we're growing closer, we really aren't because her fiancé is always there, like an invisible wall. With him so far away, she can imagine he's anything—how can I compete with that? I can't force her to see me, to return my feelings."

"Does she know how you feel about her?"

"Not in so many words." Though I hadn't spoken my feelings

aloud, I thought Harper could see them in my face, in every look and every moment we spent together. "She's engaged, remember?"

My mother gave a soft snort. "You want to know what I think?"

I didn't really, but I knew I was going to hear it anyway. "I think you are so worried about forcing yourself on her that you haven't given her a choice. Harper can make up her own mind— you should know her well enough by now to know that. But if you haven't given her any reason to believe you feel something for her, how can she know she has a choice to make?"

I scrubbed a hand over my face. "What are you suggesting?"

My mother leaned forward, her dark eyes intent. "You want to know why I broke off my engagement? Because one night we were at a ball and your father invited me to take a walk with him . . . and I accepted." She hesitated before rushing on. "He kissed me, and I knew at that moment I was engaged to the wrong man."

"He kissed an engaged woman?" I would never have imagined that of my father, who was the epitome of respect and good manners. "I don't think that will work for me. She's made it very clear that she's loyal. No matter how she feels about us, kissing me would be cheating on him."

"The kiss isn't the point, son. The point is that I *chose* to go on that walk with him. That was simply not done in those days when you were engaged. He knocked, but I opened the door. It was my choice. I'm not saying you should kiss Harper. But knock on the door, invite her to take that walk—or whatever that happens to be for her. Because if she has feelings for you, you're not doing her or her fiancé any favor by letting her walk away."

I gave a sharp nod. "I'll think about it."

"Good. Then I'll go talk to Carmen and then let myself out." She leaned forward so I could kiss her cheeks. "Good luck, son."

I stared after her as she left. What would be the equivalent of a walk for Harper, a modern American woman who saw nothing intimate in taking walks or having dinner alone with a man who was an employer and friend? What could I do that wouldn't break the trust she had with me or her commitment to her fiancé?

The sun had already set by the time I knew how to remind Harper of our connection and give her a glimpse of the future we could have together. Best of all, it wouldn't require the help of any of my live-in staff. All I needed was music and an invitation.

Harper

I threw clothes in a suitcase mindlessly. I'd take only the one. Graham and I had talked about my staying there until he had leave, but that wasn't for another two weeks, and I really wanted to see Tristan's project through.

The hour flight to the US base in Germany really meant up to three hours of traveling when you added time for driving to the airport and checking in. If it hadn't meant traveling through several countries where I didn't speak the language, I'd almost rather drive the seven hours by car. I might still end up doing that if I couldn't find an available flight. Despite Mel's offer, I wasn't going to let her inconvenience Damien with a request to use his plane. They might have money, but it wasn't mine to spend, and asking felt like taking advantage.

I sank to the padded bench inside the walk-in closet, holding one of the shimmering swimsuits Tristan had bought. Would I need it? Graham would be thrilled to see me in the water, if we could find any to swim in.

Then why did I feel a pit of dread in my stomach?

A soft knock at the door shook me from my reverie. *Our movie night.* Maybe Tristan was here to invite me, and we could forget the awkwardness and go back to being friends. I wanted that. I opened the door, expecting to see Tristan's face, his brown eyes laughing as he made some outlandish movie request. Tonight I'd let him watch whatever he wanted.

No one was outside the door. I looked up and down the hallway I'd dubbed the "middle hall," because of its medium size, but it was completely deserted. "Tristan?" I called.

No answer. I was about to shut the door when I glanced down at the carpet and spied a cream-colored envelope lying on an elaborate silver tray. I swooped up the letter, glancing again up and down the hallway as I opened it. Inside was a handwritten note on a card with Tristan's monogram.

Tristan Fontaine requests the pleasure of your company at a formal ball held tonight in the newly-redesigned Fontaine ballroom. The event is held to honor Harper Thackery for her talent and vision. Dancing will be the main feature and will begin at nine o'clock in the evening. Enclosed is a reply card, which you may leave on the silver tray.

The lettering was in Tristan's flowing cursive, and I couldn't help but smile. Nine o'clock left me only a half hour to dress. Did Mel even pack anything appropriate? I didn't know because by the time I had tried to unpack my suitcases, the housekeeper had beaten me to it.

First things first. Going back inside the room, I took out the reply card and wrote:

Harper Thackery delightfully accepts your kind invitation to attend the ball. She thanks you for holding it in her honor and especially for sparing her from Terminator 3.

Chuckling to myself, I put the card on the tray outside the door. I was tempted to listen for footsteps so I could catch Tristan retrieving it, but I didn't have much time to get ready. Besides, he might ask the housekeeper to pick it up for him.

I hurried to the closet. Of course Mel hadn't packed my gown from the last ball, which had been wise since the layers would have taken up half a suitcase, but she had packed two simpler gowns that were perfect for a night out on the town. One was my little black dress and the other a orange one with a long, full skirt and tiny glittering sequins on the shoulders. The black dress was shorter and presumably would give me better leg movement, but I knew the material was too tight. No, it would have to be the orange, which was full enough to allow decent movement.

The dress would show even small bulges, though, especially those around the waist that might signal I needed to cut back on pastries. Thankfully, Mel had known to pack my shaper that I always used with this dress. I put that on first and studied myself carefully to make sure my waist looked reasonably good.

I chose a careful twist for my long hair, wishing I had the help of Mel's hairdresser, but when I finished, no one would guess that I had resorted to using over fifty bobby pins. I applied my makeup with a heavier-than-normal hand, finishing with a faint brushing of gold glitter. Nylons and my ballroom dance shoes made the final touches.

I tried a few dance moves, and the dress allowed every step. It wasn't something I'd normally choose for serious ballroom dance because of its length, but it would do for tonight. I examined the entire ensemble in the mirror. *Not bad. Orange* was definitely my color.

All at once a hundred butterflies seemed to take wing inside my stomach. Was this a good idea? I found I really didn't care. Laughing my nervousness away, I waltzed to the door. Tristan was a gentleman, and it was only a dance to celebrate the new renovations.

The lights were burning brightly in the ballroom, and waltz music played through hidden speakers around the room. Air conditioning made the room slightly cool—perfect for dancing. Tristan stood by the door, looking amazing in a black tuxedo and orange dress shirt. In his hands he held a orange-red rose I recognized as coming from his garden.

He bowed before presenting it to me. "Thank you for coming."

"I wouldn't miss it for the world." I sniffed the rose before laying it on a table against the wall. "I like your shirt."

"I think orange is my color too." He took my hand, leading me to the middle of the floor.

His arm went around me and we began with a simple waltz, gradually adding the flourishes and variations you didn't usually see at most parties. We were good together, swaying and bending and twirling. Heat spread through me as we continued dancing. As my limbs loosened, I became more brave with my moves.

We collided as I tried a turn without waiting for his lead. His laughter rang out over the ballroom. "Good move. Let's try it again." This time he was ready, moving aside and turning gently to meet me. He swirled and dipped me as the music ended.

He eased us back to an upright position, his eyes holding mine as we waited for the next song. I couldn't look away—didn't want to look away. New music began, and we started to cha-cha, followed by the foxtrot, then the two-step.

"This music is perfect," I said when we paused to drink ice water from wine glasses on a table near the controls to the sound system.

He poured himself a second glass. "I confess, I burned it all just now on a CD while I was waiting for you to come down. One of my sisters has stacks of music in her room, all labeled nicely. Otherwise, it would have taken a week."

I turned my ear in the direction of the nearest speaker. "Is that a swing? Come on!" I set my water down and grabbed his hand.

"I'd better remove my jacket."

I helped him pull it off. Unlike at Mel's ball, there were no people to worry about running into. Country swing was one of my favorite dances because it was so sassy and fun. Neither of us was dressed for it, but we did it anyway, and when it was finished, we rewound the music and did it three more times, adding to and perfecting our moves until we were laughing so hard we had to take another water break to calm down.

"Let's do another waltz," I said. "So we can catch our breath."

He laughed. "Never thought of suggesting a dance to catch my breath, but I guess the waltz *is* much slower than the swing." He pulled me close, searing my skin with his touch.

After each dance, we separated, waiting for the music to begin again. Time slipped away, but neither of us cared. I felt I could dance all night. Or maybe for the rest of my life.

When the first strains of a tango filled my ears, I lifted my eyes to see Tristan watching me, his gaze hooded, his hands folded tightly in front of him. Slowly, he unclenched his hands and lifted them, showing me he was ready. Now there was no indication of emotion except that partial closing of his eyes, as if he didn't want me to guess what he was feeling.

But I knew what I was feeling, and I wanted to dance this with him. I stepped forward and placed my hand against his.

Tristan

She was so incredibly beautiful. My eyes drank her in, wondering if this was the last time we'd ever dance together. No. I couldn't think that way. *Think about the dance.*

The problem was, as on our first night, Harper *was* the dance. Every move, every turn, every touch of her skin filled me with fire. We came together, moving with the music, slowly at first and then with more confidence. Wherever she touched me, electricity sparked through my body. The tango was the most sensual dance in the world, and Harper had it mastered.

Each measure that passed meant one measure closer to the end of the evening, and I didn't want it to end. I had proposed a walk—this tango—and she had accepted. But did she understand what it meant?

Achingly, wonderfully, agonizingly, the dance wound to an end, the last song on the CD. The silence that followed was broken only by the sound of our breath in the suddenly still air. Our eyes

locked, and I knew that I couldn't move or I would kiss her. I felt
I *had* kissed her. But I hadn't, and she still had a choice.

Finally, with the faintest sigh, she stepped back. "That was
wonderful." She paused and added, "We'd better call it a night.
I haven't found a flight yet, and I'm not excited about driving. I
don't speak German or French, and my French is really bad."

"It's improving," I offered, though I didn't at all like the idea
of her driving across Switzerland and half of Germany by herself.

She took another step back, but there was a hint of a smile on
her lips, and her eyes were still wide and dreamy with the magic
cast by the tango. I ached to reach out to her.

Time for plan B. I knew Harper well enough to know that
despite the magic between us, she was loyal and she'd need to test
out her feelings for Graham.

But what if I lost her?

I couldn't believe that would happen. Plan B was all about
fighting for her.

"I can fly you there," I said. "Well, my pilot can. I put in a
call after dinner. He's available for mid-afternoon, if that's all right
with you."

"You don't have to do that." Her brows rose with surprise. "It's
too expensive."

"Please, let me do this for you. Consider it a bonus—and a
way to get you back here that much faster to finish my house."

She watched me through half-lidded eyes, as if considering my
plea. "Why? Why would you . . . ?"

I felt a momentary flicker of triumph because that meant she'd
understood what the tango meant. She wasn't asking why I was
lending her the plane; she was asking why I would help her run
to *him*.

"Because I want you to be sure," I said softly.

Sudden tears glittered in her eyes. "Okay. Thank you."

Without warning, she stepped forward and placed a hand on my cheek, scorching me with her touch. As if in slow motion, she reached up, her eyes locked on mine, and kissed my other cheek. My chest felt ready to burst. Mere seconds stretched unbearably as I struggled not to close my arms around her. Just when I could bear it no longer, she pulled away and walked to the door.

I watched her leave.

Going to an upstairs sitting room I was using as an office during the remodel, I sat at my computer. An email to the pilot would finalize the plans. As I typed, I shook my head at the incongruity of what I was doing. Not only was I arranging Harper's flight into another man's arms, I'd practically begged for the opportunity when all I really wanted was to fly her far away from Germany and the fiancé who could never feel about her the way I did. If he had, he would never have been apart from her this long.

A second email I typed to my secretary simply said: *Cancel my meetings tomorrow afternoon. As per our discussion earlier this evening, I am leaving town for the weekend.*

Chapter 18

Harper

The plane wasn't leaving until four in the afternoon, and Tristan was sending a driver to take me to the airport. I appreciated the offer of the plane, but a little voice in my head warned that I was taking advantage of him. I'd wanted to thank him again this morning, but even though I'd been unable to sleep past six, he'd already left the house by then.

My mind kept returning to last night. After we'd danced the tango, there was no mistaking the emotion in Tristan's eyes. I didn't dare place a name on the emotion, but seeing it both terrified and thrilled me. I was torn. Part of me wanted to stay with Tristan, to see where our relationship might go, but the part of me that loved Graham wanted only to be in his arms to prove that what I felt for Tristan wasn't real.

After lunch as I waited for the driver, Jianne and I were in the drawing room going over the minor changes I'd made the day before. "I need you to make the workmen understand," I told her, "and I'm not sure when I'll be back."

Jianne and the workers could finish up here, even if I don't return. The thought wouldn't leave my mind. If I was out of the way, maybe Jianne would reconsider her rejection of Tristan. Maybe he would be happy with her.

"Jianne," I said before I could change my mind. "About you and Tristan. Maybe you should give him another chance."

The other woman turned with my printed plans in her hands. "You don't need to worry about that," she said, her eyes barely glancing at me before turning back to the plans. "Really. I . . . my parents wanted us to marry, and he is probably the kindest man I know. He tried so hard, but I wasn't strong enough for him then."

"If you love him, you should fight for him." I would. I couldn't imagine how she'd ever let him go.

Her eyes finally rose to mine. "It's too late. He was right to break up with me."

"He broke up with you? I thought you broke up with him."

"He let everyone think that. But I'm glad he broke up with me, because for the first time I feel like I'm finding myself, thanks to him—and to you."

She took a step toward me, giving me the first hug we'd ever shared. "Besides, he never looked at me the way he looks at you. After seeing you two dance at Damien and Mel's engagement party, after seeing that kind of connection—I want that for myself. But it won't be with Tristan."

I clung to her, feeling as if I'd fallen from a very tall ladder. "I'm engaged," I whispered. "You know that."

She released me and stepped back. "Then maybe you shouldn't be."

~— 👑 —~

"Are you sure you're doing the right thing?" Mel's voice sounded worried in my ear.

"You're the one who said I should do this," I reminded her.

"I know, but you sound . . . awful. Can't you wait until I can come with you? I can go in the morning."

"No, I have to do this alone." What was I saying? I didn't even know what *this* was. "And the pilot's waving at me to board. I'll call you later."

Hanging up, I went to join the pilot. "Excuse me for the delay," he said. "I was talking to the control tower. We're good to go."

He took my suitcase from the driver and motioned for me to precede him up the stairs into the plane. I did, each step weighing a hundred pounds. Finally, I reached the top.

"There you are," said a familiar voice.

I looked over to see Tristan in one of the plane's comfortable-looking bucket seats. The weight on my feet lifted. "What are you doing here?"

He grinned. "I'm taking you to him, but you're not going alone. I still have time on the flight to make my arguments."

"You've got to be kidding."

"I believe in fighting for what I want." In a single motion he rose and stood in front of me. His fingers came up to stroke my face, trailing heat.

"That's not fair." My voice was scarcely a whisper.

His jaw tensed and his nostrils flared slightly. "Yes, it is. I can't force you to believe in us—I don't want to force you—but I don't have to make it easy for you to walk away."

"I need to do this."

He inclined his head. "I know."

Tears filled my eyes, but he didn't call me on them, reaching instead to take my suitcase from the pilot. When he returned from storing it, he was carrying a box of my favorite pastries and a bottle of wine.

Tristan had the taxi take us to the hotel I normally used, which was close to the base. He would check in for both of us while I continued on to the base to meet Graham. As I drove off, Tristan watched me, his arms folded across his chest. I understood why he'd come with me. He was doing exactly what I'd told Jianne to do—he was fighting for me, or what we could become.

At last, I forced myself to look away.

During the taxi ride, I thought of how Tristan had protected Jianne this past year, and how he hadn't taken advantage of me, though he must have sensed my weakness where he was concerned. He was obviously a trustworthy man, one who wouldn't break my heart if I chose to give it to him.

But what about Graham? I told him I'd forgiven him, but now I wasn't so sure I had. Regardless, we'd invested years into our relationship. Could I give that up?

Outside the base, I didn't have to wait long at the gate before Graham arrived to sign me in. He whooped when he saw me and pulled me into his arms, kissing me thoroughly. "I'm so glad you're here," he murmured against my lips.

I kissed him back but pulled away before we became a spectacle for the guards. After showing my passport, we were allowed through the gates and headed toward Graham's quarters.

"It will only take me a little while to change," he said. "Then we'll go out to celebrate with the guys."

I'd thought we'd spend the evening alone, but I was actually relieved. I needed time to get my bearings, to feel my way to him again. Soon we piled into someone's car and headed to a club that was full of soldiers and local girls who apparently had eyes for young Americans.

Another military girlfriend was there visiting one of Graham's roommates, but it was obvious to me that I was the only odd one out. I didn't understand the jokes or the references to shared experiences, and their loud humor took me by surprise. I knew it was only a matter of time before I became accustomed to this again. If I wanted to.

The way one of the female soldiers kept making eyes at Graham was irritating. He wasn't responding and didn't seem aware of it, but maybe his inattention to her was only because I was there. Once, I'd thought Graham would be as faithful as I was, and that was one of the reasons I'd accepted our prolonged engagement. He'd been a man I could trust. But after last month everything had changed, and I was a fool to believe it hadn't. Now I had to decide if we had a future, and my choice couldn't be based only on our old experiences, because we were different people now from when we'd become engaged a year ago. Graham's betrayal, my feelings for Tristan, and our expectations for the future had to be a part of my decision.

From the day I met him, I'd realized Graham would always be a military man like both his parents. I'd admired them and was grateful they accepted me, even while suspecting that my chosen career wasn't quite worthy of their family. Graham's father had once mentioned that I would be traveling with Graham too often to use my talents on anything but our own home, that maybe I should consider enlisting instead of pursuing design. Graham had defended me, but I always understood that my dreams would come after his. I hadn't thought it mattered, but suddenly it did.

Then there was the trust issue. Could I trust him again? Did I want to?

"I'll drive the others to the base," Graham whispered in my ear as his friends got up to dance, leaving us alone. "Then I'll take you to the hotel. I don't have to be back until the morning." He stopped and pulled me into his arms. I could taste the beer on his lips.

"Graham, stop." I pulled back. "There's something I have to tell you."

He took my hand. "What? Do you want to dance?"

"No." Would I ever be able to dance again and not think about last night?

He waited for more, leaning closer so he could hear me above the music. I had to continue. "I don't know if I can do this."

Hurt filled his eyes. "What are you saying?"

I'd do anything to wipe that pain from his face—anything but lie. "I don't know if this is what I want—us, an army life, moving around the world."

His grip on mine tightened. "It's him, isn't it? I could feel you slipping away, and I know it's my fault because I betrayed your trust. I have a lot to make up for, but I know we can—"

"It's not just him." My eyes begged Graham to understand. "I love Beaumont. I love my work. I wouldn't ask you to leave the military for me, but I still want to chase my own dreams. Can you understand that? I don't know how both our dreams can come true." I hesitated before adding, "And, yeah, I also don't know if I can trust you again."

If he had been any less of a man, he might have pushed me away or spilled hurtful words, but Graham wasn't a cruel man, and he loved me. "I am so sorry I hurt you." He moved closer. "I swear I will never let you down again. We can make this work. We just have to be committed to making it work."

I nodded slowly. "I know." Two people in love, determined to give each other happiness, could always make it if they both wanted to—and if they put their partner first. Was I willing to do that with Graham?

"Trust yourself," Mel had said, and she was right. I had to trust myself and what my heart was telling me.

Tristan

*L*etting Harper leave for the base alone was the hardest thing I'd ever done. But it was her choice, and I loved her enough not to make a scene. If not for my relationship with Jianne, I might have been tempted to push harder, but I knew that letting Harper go was the only way I could be sure she was mine.

For the first hour, I sat in the hotel bar, eating great food I couldn't taste and watching something on TV that didn't register in my mind. Then I went up to the gym and ran on the treadmill until I was ready to drop. All the while, my mind went back and forth, one minute questioning my decision, and the next sure I'd done the right thing.

After a long shower, I looked at my phone, terrified at how late it was. I'd just go down to the lobby and see if she was there.

I thought about walking down the four flights of stairs to kill more time, but I ended up waiting for the elevator instead. I might miss her if she rode up in the elevator while I was in the stairwell. Besides, after last night's dancing and the jogging tonight, my legs were rubbery and weak.

Or maybe that feeling in my legs came from knowing I'd gambled and lost.

Harper had years of history with Graham. How had I ever thought that would change in two weeks?

I waited less than a minute for the elevator door to open. My breath caught in my throat to see Harper inside, standing in the middle of the narrow space, her eyes reddened and sad. Something besides sadness also colored her expression, something I couldn't read.

"Tristan," she began, still standing there, not attempting to leave the elevator. "This is the hardest thing I've ever had to do."

"It's all right," I said, wanting to spare her the pain that sliced through my chest.

She held up her left hand, palm toward her face. It took me a few seconds to realize she was no longer wearing her ring.

The doors tried to shut between us, but I pushed them open and strode into the elevator. She met me halfway, her arms going around my neck as my impetus drove us further in to the cubical space. I kissed her. It started slow and steady, deepening by the second. I kissed her mouth, her cheeks, her eyes, her neck, crushing her to me. She pushed even closer, meeting my passion with her own. She tasted of mint and warmth and something sweet. This moment was better than I'd imagined. Deeper, fuller, with nothing standing between us. I was lost in her touch. Every nerve buzzed, as if they'd only now come to life.

I hadn't realized the elevator had gone down to the lobby until the door opened. "Oh, sorry," said an elderly gentleman in German. He winked at us. "I'll wait for the next one."

"*Danke.*" I punched the button for our floor.

"All I could think about was you and Beaumont," Harper said as the door closed. "Nothing was the same. I've changed too much, or he has. Or maybe it was never what I thought at all."

She tilted her head in her special way, the one that made me want to hold her close. "Maybe all this time, I only imagined I was in love. Because when he kissed me, I didn't feel anywhere near what I felt when I danced with you last night. Or when we swam in the pool . . . or argued about what movie to watch."

Her words dispelled any fear left in my heart. "I love you, Harper Thackery. I love you with everything in my soul." I kissed her again.

And kissed her.

And kissed her.

This time I would never, ever let go.

Epilogue

Harper

hree months later, Tristan and I stood and exchanged vows in front of our friends and family at Tristan's church. He had offered to have the wedding in America, but marrying a man who was both a prince and a duke had royal requirements, and my family and friends were only too happy to have the excuse to visit Beaumont.

Mel, of course, was my matron of honor, her own wedding to Damien having taken place two weeks earlier. Others in the bridal party included Jianne, Emerson, Tristan's sisters, our parents, some of my friends from the States, and Tristan's numerous cousins.

After the seemingly very long reception at our house, we drove off in his convertible in American style, thanks to Emerson, with tin cans tied on the back and JUST MARRIED sprayed on the doors and across rear windshield.

An hour later we drove up to the castle in Vallée de la Forêt, and Tristan carried me over the threshold, where a picnic of *jambon* sandwiches and pastries awaited us. Thanks to Emerson's engineering skills, and Jianne's help with interior decorating, we'd completed work on the castle's master bedroom, a part of the kitchen, and the grand hall that we were now calling the ballroom. I estimated that the rest of the work inside and fixing the corrosion on the exterior walls would take another two years, but for the next two weeks the work was on hiatus and the place was all ours.

Tristan carried me into the ballroom and kissed me deeply, stealing my breath away as he had every day since the elevator in Germany. Setting me down, he bowed and said, "*Duchesse de Vallée*, you look lovely this evening. May I have this dance?"

Looking at me like that, he could have anything he wanted. "Of course, *Duc de Vallée*," I said with a curtsey. "As you wish."

*R*achel Branton has worked in publishing for over twenty years. She loves writing women's fiction and traveling, and she hopes to write and travel a lot more. As a mother of seven, it's not easy to find time to write, but the semi-ordered chaos gives her a constant source of writing material. She's been known to wear pajamas all day when working on a deadline, and is often distracted enough to burn dinner. (Okay, pretty much 90% of the time.) Under the name Rachel Branton, she writes romance, romantic suspense, and women's fiction. Rachel also writes urban fantasy, paranormal romance, and science fiction under the name Teyla Branton. For more information or to sign up to hear about new releases, please visit www.RachelBranton.com.

Note from the author: Thank you for spending a little time with me in my world. I hope you'll also check out my other contemporary romances. You can find a list of all my novels at the beginning of this book. Thanks again!